THE UNITED FEDERATION MARINE CORPS' GRUB WARS

BOOK 1

ALLIANCE

Colonel Jonathan P. Brazee
USMC (Ret)

Copyright © 2017 Jonathan Brazee

Semper Fi Press

A Semper Fi Press Book

Copyright © 2017 Jonathan Brazee

ISBN-13: 978-1945743153 (Semper Fi Press)

ISBN-10: 1945743158

Printed in the United States of America

All rights reserved. No part of this book may be used or reproduced by any means, graphic, electronic, or mechanical, including photocopying, recording, taping or by any information storage retrieval system without the written permission of the publisher except in the case of brief quotations embodied in critical articles and reviews.

This is a work of fiction. All of the characters, names, incidents, organizations, and dialogue in this novel are either the products of the author's imagination or are used fictitiously.

Acknowledgements:
I want to thank all those who took the time to offer advice as I wrote this book. A special thanks goes to beta readers James Caplan and Kelly Roche for their valuable input.

Cover art by Matthew Cowdery
Graphics by Steven Novak

This book is dedicated to one of my friends, Marten Ekema. Marten retired from the British Army Catering Corps after 16 years of service due to a painful spinal. That condition kept him in pain for most of his life, and kept him almost bedridden for his last years until he passed away last month.

I only knew Marten online after he read one of my books and joined my mailing list. I not only used his name, but also his profession for a character who made appearances in several of my UFMC and UFMC Twins books.

Marten and I shared many emails over the last couple of years. I appreciated his insight, but more than that, I just enjoyed our discussions. We may have never met in person, but I appreciate our connection. I mourn his passing.

AS-419

Prologue

Chief Warrant Officer Four Mary Curnutte, the "Purple Sledgehammer," shook out her bright magenta and purple hair.

Got to look good, girl, she told herself before stepping out of the tunnel to the cheers of the 500 or so humans who'd made the journey.

She stopped for a moment, then flicked her four braids before blowing a kiss to the Spectacula, her fans.

Mary knew that some, well, *many* of her fellow gladiators didn't appreciate her showboating, but she couldn't help it, especially on today of all days. This was her chance to join the nine other gladiator aces with five kills in the ring. She could retire, and while no ace would ever want for anything, the more she could connect with the public, the more opportunities would come her way.

Gladiators had been stars since the first some 120 years ago, but it had only been over the last 60 years that advances in medicine could keep the Boosted Regenerative Cancer, the "Brick," at bay so that they could live out a full life—if they managed to survive the ring, and the Klethos d'relle usually had something to say about that. Over sixty percent of all gladiators were killed during the duels. Most of the rest were either injured and retired, had regen setbacks, or never gained the skill to be deemed worthy of combat. All gladiators were honored for their sacrifices, but the aces had a special place in humanity.

"Are you going to get to the ring, Mary, or just bask in the glow?" Cora, her second asked her.

"Ah, Cora, you need to learn how to enjoy the process," she told her second. "I'm on the cusp of history, and I want to savor the moment. When you get two more braids, you'll understand."

She didn't turn at Cora's wordless sound of frustration. Mary and Cora were best friends, closer than sisters, but their preparations for a fight were polar opposites. Mary relaxed up and to the fights, not wanting to waste mental or physical energy. She used her haka to call forth her warrior. Cora got serious from a day out, focusing her thoughts and using positive imagery to prepare. Between the two of them, they had six ring victories, so both methods seemed to work.

Not that Mary was going to let a chance to dig at her friend pass by. Trash talking didn't work against the d'relle, so Cora became her target.

She slowly walked up the path to the ring, set on a level spot on the hillside. Her opponent, "Sally Mae," knelt on the far side with 40 Klethos gathered. Her name wasn't Sally Mae, of course. D'relle went unnamed, even among the Klethos-lee. That was the human label assigned to her after her first fight almost five years and six fights prior. After over a century of war, humans still didn't quite understand how the Klethos organized their fighters, but Sally Mae seemed to be the active d'relle with the most victories.

Mary wasn't overly concerned. She'd studied holo after holo of Sally Mae's fights, and she was confident in her abilities to overcome her opponent. Only one of her fights had been against a Gladiator of note, Fiona Fell-Walsh, and that had been a close thing. Mary had mad respect for Fiona, but without false modesty, she knew she was a far better fighter than her fellow gladiator had been. Mary wasn't going to underestimate her opponent, but neither was she afraid of her.

On the near side of the ring, and running up the slope, were the assembled humans. Mary had fought in front of 100,000 on Belaster, and she had fought with only 50 humans in attendance. Of course, millions, if not billions, of people would watch the holocast safe at home.

The Klethos, on the other hand, rarely had more than 20 observers, so the 40 here was quite unusual. AS-419 had been a Klethos world at one time and won by the humans. Now, the Klethos for reasons only known to them, wanted it back. Mary was determined to keep it under human possession.

"Győzelem!" someone from the Spectacula shouted as Mary came up to the ring.

She turned and blew another kiss from the general direction of the shout. Mary was proud of her heritage, and even if she didn't speak old Hungarian, "győzelem," which meant "victory," had become a rallying cry for New Budapest gladiators.

After Tamara Veal, the *Megmentő's* victory to take back the planet a century ago, New Budapest always provided more than its share of gladiators. Despite having less than a tenth of a percent of humanity's population, no fewer than 38 of the current 347 active gladiators were daughters of the planet. The great Crystal Kovács was the first gladiator ace, although the Brick claimed her a year later.

"Győzelem," she shouted back to the delight of the crowd.

"It's time," Cora quietly said.

Mary wanted to make some smart-ass remark, but her friend was right. It was go time. She took several calming breaths and stepped to the edge of the ring before sinking into a *seiza*, or kneeling posture, hand on her thighs, eyes focused straight ahead.

The d'relle queen stood up in the typically smooth movement of their kind and strode to the middle of the ring, eyes locked on Mary for a few long moments before lifting her head back and screeching, her neck feathers flaring out. Then came the stomp, where she lifted one leg high in the air, then brought it forward, slamming it into the ground, clawed toes pointing forward as she leaned over the leg, looking back at Mary.

All d'relles started her portion of a challenge ceremony much as Sally Mae had done. Once completed, they moved into their personalized haka, and this was what Mary wanted to watch. As her opponent launched into her challenge haka with a series of whirls, each one faster than the previous, Mary studied the movements of her opponent, looking for anything that stood out that differed from the holos. More than a few gladiators had lost fights when specific d'relles showed different patterns than they'd previously shown. Sally Mae was more graceful than most, as Mary already knew, but that grace didn't come at the expense of her strength. There was also power in each stylized movement. She twirled and spun, all four arms intertwining in continual motion. Her typical Klethos cutlass looked no different than any other d'relle weapon, but it didn't sing through the air as most did. It was more as if it was slipping through the air instead of cleaving through it. With ten or twelve blindingly quick pirouettes, the d'relle kicked up a small cloud of dust before landing back in the challenge pose, one foot stretched out and pointed at Mary.

Mary didn't detect anything new in Sally Mae's haka. That didn't mean the d'relle wasn't going to try and surprise her, but it did give her a better sense of confidence.

Mary waited ten, then fifteen seconds before she slowly stood up with none of the fluid grace of her opponent. She stretched, almost languidly, making sure her shark suit was smooth against her skin. She flicked her left forefinger, the tiniest of motions, but one for which Cora was watching. Without turning around, she reached back with her right hand at the moment Cora swung Kitten down by the blade, the handle smacking right into her hand.

More than the fight itself, this had worried Mary, and the two had practiced the little handover a hundred times if they'd done it once. And it was stupid, she knew. It wouldn't somehow cow her opponent, and while it would look great in the holo, the slightest mistiming or mistake and she'd be going into the fight either cut or even missing her hand.

With that out of the way, Mary took ten steps forward until she was a meter from the motionless Sally Mae. She stood there a moment, calling forth her warrior self.

Mary considered herself a schizophrenic fighter, something Cora thought was utterly ridiculous. Part of her was a berserker, full of rage and unstoppable power. But at the same time, part of her was cool and collected, analyzing the fight and planning ahead four, five, six moves at a time.

Berserkers had power and rage to crush an opponent's defenses, but a berserker can be cut down by the quick and smart fighter. By keeping half of her mind in her analytical strategist mode, she could take advantage of her power and force of will while still fighting a cerebral battle. Cora thought it was crazy, that no one could split themselves like that and still function, but four kills in the ring rather attested to how well it worked for her.

A haka was part of the formalities of challenge and acceptance, but like most Gladiators, Mary used hers to focus. She did not dance with the style of a Celeste, nor with the historical significance of a Tamara Veal. To her, her haka had only one purpose, and that was to build the dust devil of martial will into a tornado that can't be stopped. She spun away from her opponent, yelling at the top of her voice, swinging Kitten as if to cut the sky. She stomped her feet, spun heavily, and ran to the edge of the ring and back to the center, time and time again. And it was working. Her warrior-self pushed through, coursing through her body, filling her with unstoppable strength. Kitten became a tiger in her hands, the heavy claymore ready to smash through her opponent's defenses and crush her. Her rational brain knew her tirade of a haka was spending precious energy, but she didn't care. None of her previous fights had gone past 30 seconds, and this one wouldn't, either.

Finally, when her body just couldn't contain the power any longer, she slammed her foot down in the lunge before Sally Mae, accepting the challenge.

She paused there for three full seconds before bolting back five meters, gaining a bubble of breathing room.

Now, you are mine, she told herself raising her claymore so that the tip was above her right shoulder, the pommel out in front of her belly.

Her opponent never moved and just stared at her.

OK, if that's the way you want it, sister.

With a shout, Mary started to charge, but not the headlong charge of a mindless fighter run amok. Her strategist self was active and ready for any movement, any feint, and strike, confident that she could counter anything the d'relle could throw at her and possibly return with a fatal blow. The d'relle couldn't just crouch there; she had to react, or she'd be killed.

But in warfare, the unexpected is usually the expected.

Before Mary closed the distance, the d'relle, who had been still crouching in her challenge lunge, dropped her sword into the dirt and bowed lower, forehead touching the ground and all four arms splayed as she presented her neck to the charging gladiator.

The berserker was in full rampage, and the d'relle's neck called out for the bite of Kitten.

She dropped her sword? Mary managed to wonder as she lifted her claymore for the death stroke.

Never, in the history of over 798 challenges, had a d'relle willingly give up her sword.

Mary had already started her downstroke when her strategist self pulled the stroke to the side. Something was wrong, and Mary didn't like surprises.

She could hear shouts of "Győzelem" from the Spectacula and "Mary, kill her!" from Cora, but she pulled back, still conscious of the sword beside the d'relle. She knew this could be a trick, an effort to strip her of her berserker. If so, that could be working, because she could feel the power of her warrior begin to fade. But the strategist in her realized something bigger was happening, even if she didn't know what. She kept the point of her claymore pointed the prone d'relle.

"Sally Mae," she said, clearing her throat before realizing that was only their name for her opponent. "D'relle, why have you stopped fighting?"

"Do you accept victory, Mary Curnutte?" the d'relle said in surprisingly flawless Basic.

Accept victory? She's giving up?

"Why don't you fight?" she asked again.

"Do you accept victory, Mary Curnutte?" the d'relle repeated.

There seemed to be almost a ceremonial feel to the question. Keeping the tip of her sword pointed at the d'relle, Mary looked back. Cora was urging her to kill the d'relle, the UAM officials looked concerned as several of them started forward, and the crowd started yelling out.

She looked back at the d'relle, who was sitting still, bottom hands on her knees, waiting for an answer.

God help me if I'm wrong, Mary thought.

"Yes, I accept victory," she said with a rush.

"Good. You and I must now talk."

EARTH

Chapter 1
Skylar

"Congratulations, Doctor Ybarra," the vice-minister himself said holding out his hand.

"Thank you, sir. I'm honored, and more than a little surprised, I have to admit."

"Why surprised? You're the best xenobiologist on my staff, so who should I be sending?"

Sky had made her name in xenopsychology. She knew she was the best xenobiologist in the entire ministry, as did most of her peers, but she hadn't thought that the lofty vice-minister knew her name, much less her accomplishments.

"It's just . . ." she tried to compose herself a frame a response that wouldn't make her look like an idiot. "It's just that with my lack of field experience, I'd have thought you—"

"You thought I would assign someone who's been in the field for forty or fifty years, like Madeline Sumuko, right?"

Sky blanched at the thought. Madeline had been with the ministry for almost as long as there had been a Department of Alien Affairs, and she was essentially part of the furniture. She was also stubborn, close-minded, and prone to inopportune comments. Sky could think of no one worse for the assignment. She stammered, trying to come up with a response when she saw the twinkle in the vice-minister's eye.

He's playing with me, she realized with a start.

"So, unless you think your young years renders you unqualified . . ." he said, trailing off in a question.

"Oh, no, sir. I can do it. I know I can."

"I know you can, too, Doctor Ybarra. That's why I chose you, and I'm not used to having my subordinates questioning that."

Sky started to protest that she wasn't questioning him, but the twinkle was still there. He was simply having his fun.

"Far be it from me to do that, sir. I trust your judgment implicitly," she said, playing along.

"Good to hear. Well, I need to get back to my desk. You've got five days to prepare, and I expect most of that will be in meetings, so don't let me keep you."

"Right, sir. And thank you, sir," she said, understanding that she'd been dismissed.

The vice-minister turned away and took a step before turning back to her. "Skylar, I was 23 years old on Porcelain. I thought I was in over my head, but, I think it turned out OK. You'll do well, too. Just remember, you are the Ministry's rep in the field, so don't let the military or the First Ministry push you around, much less the UAM, OK?"

Sky knew the story of Porcelain, where the vice-minister, then brand new to the Second Ministry and on his first assignment, almost single-handedly averted a planetary war. She felt a surge of confidence. If he thought she could do it, then she knew she could.

"Thank you, sir. I won't let you down."

"I know you won't. So," he said, holding out his hand again. "Kick some ass for us, OK?"

"Yes, sir!" she said, shaking his hand.

She watched him try to wend his way out of the conference room, only to be stopped by three people with something vital that he had to address. That was life as a Federation vice-minister, never a free moment, yet he had just spent several of those moments with her. Skylar Ybarra, a lowly FS12 Junior Counsellor from the backwater planet of Nuevo Monterrey.

FS15, she reminded herself with a little surge of pride.

Being assigned as the Second Ministry Advisor to the task force came with an FS15 rank, on par with a Navy captain or Marine Corps colonel. She looked over the the military men and women as they huddled, listening to Admiral Xu.

How many of them are going to treat me as an equal? she wondered.

Sky had enough problems within her own department. Her credentials were impeccable. She'd graduated magna cum lade from EEU at the age of 19, then earned her Ph.D. from the Earth campus of Oxford three years later. Her dissertation, *Implications of Klethos-lee Aggression Sublimation*, had won the Propov Award and was considered the new gold standard for Klethos psychology. Turning down lucrative academic and business positions, she'd joined the Second Ministry, anxious to make her mark in the world, but she'd discovered that not everyone appreciated bright young stars disturbing the status quo. It had taken her two years of publishing impeccable work and more than a little ass-kissing to be accepted. And now, at 25 years old, she was the de facto Federation xeno-expert to the UAM mission.

And the reason for the mission stood quietly to the side of the room, observing the humans, but seemingly ignored. Not to Sky, though. Her dissertation might be the gold standard, but no one really knew the Klethos, not even after 120-plus years. Their introduction of the d'solle, a new class of Klethos, and evidently ay a type of leadership class, had taken humanity by surprise, for example.

"Sally Mae's" voluntary defeat in the ring, and the subsequent revelation that the Klethos faced an inter-galactic enemy, one that could threaten the entire galaxy, had been more of a shock. The Klethos wanted allies, pure and simple, and over a century of styled warfare with humans had convinced them that they would fit the bill.

As a xenobiologist, Skylar was familiar with the sad story of the Trinoculars, which was why she gravitated towards the study of the still-enigmatic Klethos. Now, to find out there was still another intelligent species out there, one more powerful and advanced, Sky was excited and yearned to learn more. Not everyone shared her excitement.

A growing percentage of humanity wanted nothing to do with the request for assistance. The Klethos were a powerful race, able to sweep aside humanity if it weren't for the single-warrior challenges. If there were a more powerful race out there, a more aggressive race, then they wanted nothing to do with them. Over the last four months, debate within the UAM in furtive, international discussions, raged.

Sky wasn't militarily-minded, but to her, the answer was a no-brainer. If there was a threat out in the black, then humanity had better learn all they could about it. They couldn't do that putting their collective heads in the sand and hoping to scoot by unnoticed.

In the end, the UAM task force was authorized, not to join the fight, but to try and get a grasp of the situation. The overall mission commander was the UAM's Second Secretary, Archbishop Lowery from the Brotherhood. The task force's military commander was the Federation's Admiral Xu.

The Brotherhood and the Federation made up the bulk of the task force, with the Confederation of Free States, Greater France, and some independents such as New Budapest and Outback filling the remaining roster spots.

Sky felt eyes on her and broke her gaze from the Klethos. She scanned the room to spot Dr. Peyton Janus staring at her. He nodded, then broke contact with her. Dr. Janus was the UAM xenobiologist, not actually Sky's boss but higher on the food chain than her. He was a citizen of the Alliance of Free States, which was not participating in the task force, so he was there as an officer of the UAM. Sky had never met the man before the start of the conference the day before, but she had read his work. She hadn't been too impressed.

Doesn't matter. I report to Executive Counsellor Baker and Admiral Xu, not him.

She wasn't going to avoid him, and maybe they could work together, but nothing was going to get in her way of learning everything she could about the Klethos.

FSS BENJAMIN GRABOWSKI

Chapter 2
Hondo

"Did you see that lady scientist?" Sam asked.

"Which one?" BK asked as she honed her combat knife.

"The good-looking one, with the dark hair."

"You mean the xeno-lady? Yeah, I saw her. What about her?" she asked, raising the blade and squinting one-eyed to check the edge.

"Pretty hot, huh? I bet she's a wild one out on the town, you know? I might have to look her up if we ever pull libbo on this mission."

"Oh, shit, Sam. You know you aren't man enough for her. Let me have a chance, though, and I'll take her to wonderland. She'll never want to come back."

"You think so? Like that bartender on Once More, right? Yeah, she was sure into you, right?" He turned away from her and asked, "Hey, Hondo isn't that right?"

Lance Corporal Hondo McKeever, United Federation Marine Corps, looked up from his novel and asked, "What is right?"

"That bartender on Once More, the one that BK was hitting on. She shot BK down in flames, right?"

Hondo rolled his eyes and went back to his book without answering. Lance Corporal BK Dodds and Private First Class Sam Gelhorn were his two closest friends in the squad—which was a good thing as they made up three-fourths of Second Fire Team. BK and Sam were usually going at it like, well, like brother and sister.   That was kind of appropriate, he guessed. The three of them, four, if you counted Corporal Yetter, were a family of sorts. They bickered and quarreled, but they loved each other with a bond that couldn't be broken.

BK and Sam, in particular, gave each other a ration of shit. They each had a competitive streak a klick long, and if it wasn't range scores or bench presses, it was trying to bed the most attractive woman wherever they were at.

Hondo smiled at the memory of Once More. Both BK and Sam were hitting on a bartender who was obviously not the slightest bit into either one of them, but under the influence of Mr. Jack, both chose to see interest where none existed. He, on the other hand, had made the acquaintance of an older woman who seemed to like men in uniform, and while those two preened like courting birds, Hondo had slipped out of the bar for a very mutually enjoyable few hours. He'd never told his two mates what he'd been doing, and as he escorted their drunk asses back to the liberty shuttle, they both berated him for being so boring.

Well, "boring" wasn't going to be a problem on this mission. Third Battalion, Sixth Marines, had been pulled as part of the Sixth Marine Expeditionary Brigade, the main element of the UAM's Klethos Exploratory Relief Force. It still seemed almost inconceivable to him.   He'd watched the Gladiator duels on the holos, of course, so he'd seen Klethos queens. But now, to be on the same side? Hell, there were four Klethos onboard the *Big Ski* right now. Hondo hadn't seen any of them yet, but he was hoping to get a glimpse of one, at least.

BK and Sam were now going on about her combat knife. This was an old argument, on whether a PICS Marine needed to carry a metal blade. Sam thought it was ridiculous while BK felt it was better to be prepared in case she had to molt in the middle of a battle.

    Hondo shook his head and went back to his book. He had a feeling that down-time like this was going to be a precious commodity in the coming months.

UNNAMED PLANET

Chapter 3
Hondo

"Do you think we're going to see action?" BK asked on the fire team net.

"You were there at the ops brief," Corporal Yetter responded. "Your guess is as good as mine, so let's just focus on our mission."

"Just wondering," BK said.

Hondo was "just wondering," too. Along with everyone else, he'd been excited when they'd been diverted. Instead of Purgamentium, the ex-Confed planet that had long been in Klethos control where they were going to try and develop basic Human-Klethos tactics, they were going to an actual active planet, deep into Klethos space.

The rumor circulating among the Marines was that Admiral Xu argued against the mission, stating they were not ready to operate alongside the Klethos, but she'd been overruled by the UAM brass. Too many governments were suspicious of the Klethos' motives, and the UAM wanted proof as to the threat.

"And if proof means getting the brigade wiped out, that's a small price to pay," Corporal Yetter had muttered when Lieutenant Silas had given them the orders.

The fact that neither the lieutenant nor Staff Sergeant Aster had chastised Yetter was telling to Hondo. They must have been thinking the same thing. Marines believed that sweat in training saved lives in war, and while the brigade represented the finest the Corps had to offer, they had not even cross-trained yet with the Brotherhood Host, the Confederation Legion, or any of the smaller units in the task force, much less with the Klethos.

Hondo checked his display as he kept up the pace, his PICS working smoothly. Kilo, which had been the battalion's PICS company, was leading the way through the alien landscape. The other companies followed in a rough diamond, surrounding the UAM civilians. All Marines were trained in PICS, of course, but half of the battalion had been in straight-leg platoons, only being issued their PICS aboard the *Big Ski*. PICS were all supposed to be the same, but Marines knew that each combat suit had its own personality, so for many of the battalion's Marines, their first test drive of their PICS was into a hot zone.

"What do you think? We gonna get some action?" BK asked him on the P2P.

The orders had been to keep comms to a minimum. No one knew the Grubs' capabilities in intercepting then, but enough had been passed so far that Hondo didn't think anything more would make much of a difference.

"I don't know. We're just supposed to escort the civs close enough so they can gather data, and all of that's going to be at a distance. So, maybe not."

"Too bad. I want to squeeze one of them until it pops."

That was so BK. She talked a big talk, but with her, she also walked the walk. If anyone were going to do it, it would be her. Hondo was just glad she was in his fire team.

He really wasn't sure why the civilian team needed to be on the ground. There were five ships in orbit, including a Brotherhood *Caleb-class* surveillance ship, whose scanners were second to none. The task force had thousands of drones. If the Grubs had the Klethos worried enough to seek an alliance with humanity, then Hondo thought they should gather all the information they could before they got within reach of the things.

But who cares what a lance corporal thinks? he mused, probably as foot soldiers had been doing since Babylonian times.

Sam thought it was more for show, to let both the Klethos and the rest of humanity see that they were in it for keeps. Hondo didn't know about that, and he didn't dwell on things above his paygrade—which would only be a sure ticket for an ulcer.

He looked to the right and behind where the group of six civilians marched uncertainly in the middle of the battalion, clad in Confederation sheath MRF armor. There'd been talk about getting them in a PICS or Rigaudeau-6, but that had been a pipe dream. It took a Marine three weeks to simply learn how to move in their combat suit and a French Legionnaire almost two months for a Rigaudeau-6. Leading the civilians was a Klethos quad and their liaison, a Marine major. Hondo had finally seen a Klethos in the flesh, and he had to admit they were far more intimidating in person than when on a holo next to a Gladiator.

First Platoon, which was acting as point for the battalion, started up a rise. On the other side was a broad plain, more than seven klicks across. Across the plain at the base of the low hills, the Klethos were engaged. Hondo didn't have access to the more detailed feeds that the commanders had, but his low-res feed showed signs of battle. Flashes of light and explosions could be clearly seen, and he thought he could make out the bulky white shapes of the Grubs.

"Look at the Klethos," Sam passed. "They're getting antsy."

And they were. Hondo wasn't a scholar of Klethos psychology, but they looked like they were ready to fight. It wasn't just their neck crests, which were splayed out to the fullest, but their almost trembling posture reminded him of dogs eager to be released on the hunt.

"Second, we're proceeding to the military crest on the far side and taking a position alongside First Platoon," the lieutenant passed on the platoon net while inputting the position on each Marine's display. "We are not here to engage, so unless we're attacked, all weapons systems are to be kept in the safe mode. Got it? I want acknowledgments, people."

Hondo blinked his acknowledgment, and a moment later, the entire platoon had.

"I guess we aren't getting any action," BK said on the team circuit.

"Quiet. Listen to the lieutenant," Corporal Yetter admonished her.

"If anything does go down, our orders remain the same. We're to get our protectees out of danger," the lieutenant passed.

"Protectees," Hondo thought to himself. *Nice term for us being babysitters.*

A Marine in a PICS could run at close to 50 KPH, far faster than any of their civilian charges in their Confed body armor, which was light and durable but gave no assist to movement. If things went to shit, the Second Platoon Marines were to physically pick up the civilians and carry them to the waiting shuttles six klicks back and around a low hill, or, if the situation allowed for it, to let them climb onto the PICS' hip flanges, holding onto the handles on the back. The plan seemed rather chaotic to Hondo, and the "rehearsal" consisted of practicing picking up the civilians a few times in the Big Ski's shuttle bay, to everyone's laughter and amusement.

Hondo kept marching forward in the weird landscape. He'd never been on a non-terraformed world, so normally his curiosity would have him soaking it all in, but with his pulse rising, his focus was on the crest in front of him, or rather what was on the far side of the plain. When he finally crested the top, he went to full mag to the battle ahead . . .

. . . and he saw a Grub laying waste to the Klethos around it, a blue-white light flashing and and reaching out from it.

Hondo had seen the few recordings made available to humanity what a Grub looked like, but this was different. He was seeing one of them in action.

No one knew exactly what the Grubs used as their weapons, but theories abounded. All Hondo could see was light, but not the light of a laser. It seemed to reach out slow enough for the eye to discern the movement, and not on a laser-like straight line-of-sight. The fingers of light zapped out to hit Klethos or the ground, but without explosions.

That wasn't to say he didn't see explosions at all. A huge blast erupted from the side of the Grub, but that didn't seem to faze it. Either the thing had some amazing shielding, or it was inherently tough as nails.

At seven klicks from the fight, Hondo was too far away to pick up much detail, even at full magnification. He had no idea as to the size of the battle, nor could he make out many of the Klethos.

"Look at the size of that thing," Sam passed, voicing what Hondo and probably every other Marine were thinking.

"Stop here," Corporal Yetter passed. "But be ready to shift if we get the order.

A PICS can go prone, but that entailed switching off the gyros and was a royal pain to do, and at seven klicks from the fight, the Marines felt comfortable standing. Hondo checked his power-level, glanced to where the civilians were massing and pulling out different types of what had to be sophisticated scanners, then turned back to the far side of the plain. The

Grub was no longer in sight, but there were flashes of light that flickered among what served as trees on this planet.

"Do not fire, I repeat, do not fire," someone shouted over the command net.

"Hold your fire," Sergeant Mbangwa, Hondo's squad leader repeated. "Keep your freaking systems on safe."

Hondo did a quick combat scan, hand hovering over his arming switch, wondering what was going on when he saw the Klethos quad bolting forward, a Marine in PICS that had to be their liaison, in full pursuit.

"They're joining the battle," Hondo passed on the fire team circuit in amazement.

A Marine in a PICS was fast, but the Klethos were just as quick, their relatively thin legs bounding them forward like ungodly ostriches. The major was never quite able to close the distance as they crossed the relatively flat terrain.

"The brass is probably shitting bricks right now," BK said. "Do you think that major just took off on his own like that?"

"I bet he did," Sam said. "We're not supposed to engage."

"Fucking awesome if he did. I've got to give him mad props for an O."

Hondo wasn't sure a major would simply take it on his own to enter the battle zone, but stranger things have happened before.

"Kilo Company, nothing has changed. We're still on an observational mission," Captain Montgomery, the company commander passed.

Hondo knew he should be scanning for any threat, but he couldn't help but watch the quad and the major run. It took them over eight minutes to cross the open area, and just as they reached the other side, four fingers of light reached out to envelope each of the Klethos. It was difficult to make out what exactly was happening, but to Hondo, it looked like two of the Klethos went down. There wasn't any doubt, though, when the major fired. A string of 20mm grenade fire, tracers clearly visible, reached up to a Grub as it came into view. The fire hit true, to the cheers of some of the Marines, but instead of blowing apart, the Grub shifted into a previously unknown gear and darted forward, too quickly for something of its bulk.

Lights reached out as if from a Tesla ball as it charged the major and the remaining two Klethos. Like an aura, light surrounded the major, and after a moment, the 20mm fire ceased.

The first human casualty of the war had just fallen, and Hondo swallowed hard to push down the lump that had just formed in his throat.

The Grub raised itself higher, and Hondo could swear it turned its attention on the battalion arrayed across the ridge. A finger of light zig-zagged toward them, only to peter-out, if light could do that, a klick short of the lead Marines.

"What now? We going to fire?" BK asked.

The Marines with the Weapons Pack 3 could reach across the seven klicks, and that meant Hondo. He was the fire team's missileman, his HM-48 more than capable of reaching the Grub. Somehow, the thing had taken the full brunt of the major's 20mm gun, but Hondo's 48 could take out any tank known to man. Additionally, on station 30 klicks to the rear, were two Falcon-Cs, the most powerful atmospheric craft in the Federation Marines, matched only by perhaps the Confed Orcus. Each Falcon could level a fortified city or take out a battalion of tanks.

"Stand by," Lieutenant Silas passed, her voice calm and collected.

An instant later, the Grub started forward, followed by eight or nine more that emerged from the battlefield. In a rough line abreast, the things, as big as busses, seemed to glide over the ground as they rushed the Marines.

"Kilo, Echo, engage MH-48s. Weapons Company, weapons free," the order came over the battalion ops net.

Hondo activated his weapons system. Unlike Weapons Company, which would fire at will and at any target, the line company Marines were each given a designated target. Hondo's was the second Grub from the left, and he targeted the thing as it closed the gap, already covering more than a klick.

"Get some, Hondo," BK said on the P2P. "I mean it. Those things are coming on fast."

He ignored her as his system confirmed the lock, then he triggered the missile. The next one was cycling into firing position as he watched the track of the 80cm-long missile. If the things had jamming of some sort, it didn't work, and the missile flew true, hitting the Grub on its left side an instant before another hit it right in the front. Hondo wanted to shout in victory, but the Grub barely slowed down, if at all. His missile looked as if it penetrated the thing's body, but with no effect.

There were explosions as Weapons Company's field guns struck the Grubs, and with a huge crackling of light, the beams of one of the company's energy guns hit and splashed around an advancing Grub.

Hondo fired his second missile, not seeing if any of the Marines' weapons were having an effect. One of the Falcons swooped in, its telltale broadcasting to the Marines that it was a friendly as it unleashed the fires of Hades upon the Grubs. One Grub slowed to a stop as tendrils of light from the others seemed to converge and then shoot forward as a single beam to envelope the plane. A Falcon had fairly robust shielding which was particularly effective against energy weapons, but that was no match for the Grub power. The Falcon swerved to the side in a death spiral.

And then the Grubs turned their weapons to the Marines on the ground.

Fingers of light reached out to sweep the Marines, and where the light hit, Marines were killed. The PICS armor, perhaps the best ever developed, could stand up to the onslaught for perhaps five seconds, no more.

"Cease firing, Second. Pick up your protectee and get them back to the rally point," Lieutenant Silas ordered.

Hondo had four more missiles, and he wanted to expend them, but orders were orders. Along with the rest of the platoon, he peeled back and sprinted to the civilians, his armored feet chewing up the loose soil. He'd been assigned Dr. Hastert, a UAM scientist of some sort, but the civilians were in panic mode, and the Doctor wasn't responding.

"Just pick up anyone," Staff Sergeant Aster ordered.

Evidently, Hondo wasn't the only one having trouble. Two civilians were standing in shock, looking out towards the still advancing Grubs when a finger of light reached them, hitting the man in the chest. The Confed sheath armor didn't give much protection, cracking open as the man fell.

The woman took a step back in horror, not even seeing Hondo as he stepped forward and picked her up by her waist. He turned just as his alarms went crazy and light streamed around him in goblets.

Five seconds!

The woman went limp in his arms as he triggered superman mode and jumped forward. He landed and immediately triggered another jump, this time clearing the crest. His alarms went off, flashing lights indicating the extent of the damage. He could still move, but his suit wasn't in good shape.

Staff Sergeant Aster was acting as traffic cop, getting the platoon on the move. Hondo shifted the woman to the crook of his arm, using it as a chair, which had been determined as the most comfortable way for the civilians to be carried if they couldn't mount themselves on a PICS' back. The woman wrapped her arms around his big mechanical one, which was a relief. She was still alive.

The second Falcon-C screamed overhead as it joined the battle. Hondo didn't bother to look. He felt bad for abandoning the fight. Marines were dying, but he was running for safety. His orders were clear, though, and his charge was the woman perched on his arm. Lima and Mike Companies would hold off the Grubs while Kilo got all the civilians to safety . . . hopefully. From what little Hondo had seen, he wasn't sure the rest of the battalion could stop the things.

With Third Platoon providing security, the platoon ran silently towards the rally point where the *Big Ski's* shuttles waited.

Chapter 4
Skylar

Sky held onto the Marine's arms, trying to buffer the jolting. The armor she'd been given to wear was some help, but the bottom pelvic plate dug into her with seemingly every step the Marine took.

All of this was in a fog, though. She knew she was in shock. She'd just seen Baylor Torgenson killed right in front of her eyes, for the love of God. One moment, they were watching the Dictymorph approach, and the next moment, the light tendrils enveloped him. Sky knew she would have been next if the Marine hadn't plucked her from the ground and used his bulk as a shield. Even so, her left arm was burned as if by acid, pain radiating in waves, making her nauseous as well.

Reality had just hit her across the head. She'd been so proud to be selected for the mission, representing the Second Ministry. The youngest scientist in the task force, she'd hoisted that as a badge of honor. Not only would she get to delve into the psyche of the Klethos, but she would be on the ground floor of Dictymorph study. Her career was set, and there was no telling how far she could go.

But . . . this? Somehow, despite knowing the Dictymorphs and the Klethos were at war, it never really sunk in what that meant. She'd been as vocal as anyone else when the Admiral hadn't wanted to allow them onto the planet's surface, and she'd rejoiced when Archbishop Lowery had overturned her. They were on a quest for knowledge, and no turf-protection from the military was going to get in the way of science.

The time spent on the ship with the Klethos quad had been somewhat frustrating. Each of the Klethos spoke excellent Standard, and every sentence made sense on its own. It was when everything was taken in its totality that things began to get confusing. For all their talk about honor and the warrior spirit, they seemed to know next to nothing about their enemy. Sky thought that if anything, they respected the Dictymorphs.

With the frustration mounting, Sky had jumped on the opportunity to join the party on the surface. She was sure that if she could see the Klethos in a more natural environment, that would give context to what they said. It would also give her the first data to be gathered on the Dictymorphs.

But it had gone so horribly wrong. The Dictymorphs were monsters, horrors, worse than she could have imagined. And they were deadly.

Sky wanted to look around the Marine to see if the Dictymorphs were following, but she couldn't. If she was about to die, she didn't want to see her death coming to claim her.

Next to her, Dr. Janus was being carried by another Marine. Their eyes met, and he nodded with a look of acceptance? Resignation? Sky couldn't tell. She wondered how many of her peers made it out of the battle.

The Marine carrying her started to slow down, and that was rougher as he adjusted his stride to come to a stop. Sky looked up to see the glorious sight of three shuttles, lights on and ready to take off.

Sky was sitting on his left arm, and he reached with the right to lift her to the ground.

"Are you OK, ma'am?" he asked through his external speakers.

"Uh . . . yeah, I think so. My arm's burnt, but I think so. Thank you."

"You'll get treatment onboard, ma'am."

Sky let go of his arm and saw the Marine's name which was engraved on his left chest piece.

"What's your first name, McKeever?" she asked.

"Lance Corporal Hondo McKeever, ma'am."

"Well, thank you, Hondo. Can I call you that?"

"It's Lance Corporal McKeever, ma'am," he told her.

"OK, Lance Corporal. I just want to thank you. You saved my life."

"Just doing my job, ma'am," he said, his voice sounding sorry despite coming through a speaker.

Why is he sorry? He got away from that madness. He lucked out.

"What's now? Do we get on the shuttles?"

"You get on the shuttles, not us."

"But you've got to get out of here, too."

"Not while we have Marines back there, ma'am, still fighting so you can get back to the ship."

Sky wanted to argue, to say that "back there" was hopeless. She appreciated their sacrifice, but any rational person would understand that at this point, nothing more could done.

She was about to say that when McKeever said a final, "You'd better get going," and turned around. It was only then that she saw all the Marines had turned as well and were going back to the battle.

That's crazy!

"Come on, Doctor Ybarra. We've got to get on the shuttle," Dr. Janus said, grabbing her arm.

Sky yelped as the remnants of the armor dug into her burned arm. Still, she let the head xenologist lead her to join the others as they loaded. One step onto the ramp, she stopped to look back. The Marines were already 200 meters away, rushing to the sound of gunfire.

She shook her head in disbelief and boarded her lifeboat back up to the ship.

FS BENJAMIN GRABOWSKI

Chapter 5
Hondo

A blue beam sliced from out of the recorder's field of view, hitting the Grub dead on with kilojoules of energy. The Grub recoiled, raising the front half of its body while tendrils of light shot out, only to be wisped out like a blown candle. Explosions rocked the creature, taking out chunks of the white flesh. With a shudder, the Grub collapsed, its carcass spreading out as gravity took hold of it.

Hondo suppressed a cheer—too many had been lost to celebrate anything.

"As you can see, the Grubs can be killed," the Navy commander said. "The fire that immobilized it came from the Confederation destroyer, the *CS Philippi*. The meson beam was depicted in blue for this brief, of course, but its effectiveness can't be denied. With the *Philippi's* help, four of the Grubs were killed."

"Yeah, and the *Philippi* was shot out of orbit, too," Tinman said from his bunk.

"They're just trying to show that we can kill the bastards, so lay off of them," BK said.

The nonrates in the squad, who had somehow come out of the battle intact, were sitting in berthing, watching the brief. Most of the Marines who survived were in some degree of shock. In less than an hour on the surface of the planet, 68% of the battalion had been wiped out. Mike Company, which had taken the brunt of the attack, had only four survivors. No other Marine battalion, going back to the War of the Far Reaches had lost so many in a single battle.

"And now we're looking at another Grub kill, this one when the Klethos pursued them."

Hondo had seen this with his own eyes, returning to the ridge just as the mass of Klethos fighters reached the Grub. At least forty Klethos had converged on it, some firing their disrupter rifles into the massive body while others fired what looked to be wide-mouthed anti-boarding guns that shot out metallic objects big enough and moving slow enough to be picked up in the holo. Instead of simply aiming at the center mass, though, they seemed to focus on one portion of it while the thing "fired" tendril after tendril of the plasma-like light, killing or disabling the Klethos with each swipe. A chunk of the thing finally sloughed off, and Hondo took the opportunity to fire an HM-48 into the wound. As before, the missile simply disappeared into the Grub's body, but Hondo thought it had to have done some good.

Then came a line of Klethos who rushed the Grub bearing what looked to be Roman lances or pikes. Swinging them, lights and sparks flashed off the tip as either the pikes' or the Grubs energy fields were disrupted. More Klethos fell, but at last, whether from their efforts of the massed fire from the Marines, the Grub collapsed to the ground like a half-filled water balloon, as if its skin could no longer support its mass.

"With this kill, that made six. Three Grubs broke off the assault and fled the battlefield," the commander continued as if that constituted a victory.

Any more victories like that will be the death of us.

None of the Marines who'd been on the ground thought it was much of a victory. Too many friends had been lost, all to kill six Grubs. Another hundred or so Kelthos littered the battlefield. The Marines had gone in confident, even eager for a fight, but the stark reality of why the Klethos wanted allies was abundantly clear.

"And now, if I can ask Doctor Ybarra to give us an info-dump on what we've discovered about the Grubs so far. Doctor Ybarra?"

The woman Hondo had carried out of the battle stepped forward, looking much smaller—and much younger—out of her armor. Her left arm was in a regen sleeve.

"Hey, it's the xeno-lady," Sam said, but no one was in the mood to comment.

"Thank you, Commander," she said before clearing her throat. "Um . . . we still don't have a detailed analysis of just what we're facing here. We took tissue samples of the dead Dictymorph, samples of the residue of their weapons," she continued, her right hand drifting to rub the regen sleeve. "The tissue sample is being broken down to send the data to every lab of the allied governments. I can tell you this, it's nothing we've seen before. It is not carbon-based; that we've already determined. But just what kind of life this is, we'll need more time for that. The weapon they used, though, is some sort of a chemical weapon. The molecular structure had both similarities to luciferase, one of the three ingredients that enable bioluminescence, and some acids. But that's too general a comparison, as you can see from here."

A convoluted-looking molecule appeared on the monitor, parts of it highlighted. Alongside of it, two other molecules, one labeled luciferase and the other luciferin, were displayed. Dr. Ybarra, started going into detail that quickly went beyond Hondo's understanding or care.

"I don't care what it is, lady. You just tell us how to kill it," BK said to the mutters of agreement of the other eight Marines in the compartment.

Even the commander looked glassy-eyed ten minutes later when the woman finally stopped explaining. Despite all the science being thrown about, as far as Hondo could tell, all they knew was that the thing was not like life as humans understood it. Everything else was a mystery. The only thing she'd said that had resonated was that the best scientists in human space were working on deciphering the Grubs, or Dictymorphs, as she called them, so they could develop weapons that would kill them.

Admiral Xu was the last person to speak. She looked much older than she had a week ago when she welcomed the units to the fighting arm of the task force. She'd been put into a tough position, having to implement a plan that she had fought against. It turned out she was right. Right or not, however, losing a Confederation ship and the bulk of a Federation Marine battalion was not something that she was going to be able to overcome. In the old days, she'd face execution. Today, she'd be retired in disgrace and unofficially exiled to some backwater planet. Some people would say that execution would be more merciful.

"Sailors, Marines, soldiers, and Legionnaires of the task force, I just want to tell you how proud I am of your performance. You did your duty no matter what faced you."

"Not everyone. Just us in 3/6 and the Confed ship. The rest just watched," BK said, pointing out the obvious.

"You suffered great losses, but those losses were not in vain. With the data we gathered, we'll be able to develop weapons and tactics that will allow us to come back and defeat this new enemy."

Pretty high price to pay for that, Hondo thought, despite his knowing that she was right.

With just under 1,100 dead, the price was a relatively cheap one to pay in the grand scheme of things to get the information they needed. There had been naval battles over the last 200 years that had killed hundreds of thousands. The difference was, at least to him, that he knew many of those killed, fellow Marines who had no chance at resurrection. Marines with whom he'd gone to boot camp. Two Marines from his home planet of Paradhiso. Marines and corpsmen from the battalion with whom he'd played sports with and against, whom he'd shared beers on liberty. Friends.

Hondo thought about those who were gone, the admiral's words fading away until her "We've got our new orders," dragged him back to the present. Everyone wanted to know what was next, and over 4,000 sets of ears on the four remaining ships were locked on what she would say next.

"We've been ordered to Purgamentium to train up, as per our original orders. This will include combined training with the Klethos. Human forces will not be committed until we are an integrated force and have weapons that will kill Grubs."

Hondo was both disappointed and relieved. He was disappointed because the seed of hate had been planted in his heart. He wanted to kill every Grub that dared stick its whatever it had for a head in human space. But he was also relieved. He knew the task force was not ready to fight the Grubs. It wasn't just their weapons. The task force was just too disjointed. Each force was the best that their governments could provide, but that didn't mean they could operate together yet, much less alongside the Klethos. And if the battle has shown anything, it was that weapons designed to take out combat soldiers and tanks were not effective against the Grubs.

"You will have a new commander upon our arrival on Purgamentium," the admiral said, looking defeated despite her erect posture and firm voice. "But you can rest assured that I'll be with you in spirit. You have all done me proud."

The brass that was with her in the conference room stood up and applauded while she slowly saluted them, then turned to the holo pickups. She held the salute for too long, then cut away before stepping off the platform. Brigadier General Reicker, the task forces' second-in-command and senior Confederation military rep, stepped up and said, "Commanders, take charge of your units and carry out your orders."

"So, we go get to do cross-training? For what?" Loren deSpiri asked, her voice bitter.

"So we can crush the Grubs," BK said.

"Yeah, and how're we gonna do that by cross-training? You saw what they did to us, and to the Klethos, too. No training's gonna make us into super-Grub killers, you know."

BK opened her mouth as if to answer, but kept silent. Hondo could feel the atmosphere in the compartment chill.

"The Capys, they seemed invincible," he blurted out.

"What?" several voices asked at once.

"The Capys, when we first found them, they seemed invincible."

"Bullshit," BK said. "The fucking Capys?"

Hondo understood their incredulity. The Capys, or Trinoculars, were a sad testimony of what could happen to a species. Relegated to a few reservations on human worlds, there were probably fewer than 100,000 left alive. In popular culture, they were a dying race, owing their continued existence to humanity.

But it hadn't always been that way. When the two species first interacted, the Capys had sent the humans packing.

"No, it's true. On G.K. Nutrition Six, that's where we first met. They wiped out a Marine battalion and almost a second. Ryck Lysander was there."

"Oh, yeah, that's where he got his first Nova, right?" Brute asked.

"Not quite. He got it on HAC-440, but yeah, it was against the Capys. Hell, he killed one of them with a freakin' grappling hook."

"How do you know all of this?" Sam asked.

"I read. Maybe you should try it."

"If the Capy's were so tough, then why are they all gone now?"

"They weren't that tough. We just didn't know how to handle them yet. Once we understood them, once we knew what made them tick, it was all over. They couldn't stand up to us."

"Or to the Klethos. That's why they came into our space in the first place, right?" BK asked.

"Yeah, right. They were between two more aggressive races, and they couldn't compete," Hondo said.

"So how are the Capy's and the Grubs related? I mean, look at the differences," Loren asked.

"They're not exactly related. But what is related is that the key is understanding the things. Once we do that, nothing can stand in our way."

The small berthing compartment was silent as the Marines digested what they'd heard. Hondo knew that Marines like BK were hyped up to take the attack to the Grubs, to punish them. He knew that others like Loren were not as confident given what the battalion had just gone through. He understood those feelings. But he also understood why they'd been ordered to Purgamentium.

The Grubs were a threat to mankind. He was sure of that. They weren't ready, they hadn't been ready, to fight them. They couldn't go into battle half-cocked simply for political reasons. The next time they faced the Grubs, and Hondo was sure there would be a next time, they had to be ready to kick some Grub ass.

PURGAMENTIUM

Chapter 6
Hondo

"Hell!" Sergeant Mbangwa shouted, his voice full of frustration. "There they go again. Keep up with them."

"You heard the man," Corporal Yetter said. "Let's go round them up."

The entire squad bolted forward at max speed, trying to run down the Klethos. They were in full berserker mode and running all out, so the Marines were just able to keep the eight Klethos in sight as they ran across the rubble-strewn ground.

"Don't let them draw their fucking swords," the sergeant passed.

Like we can stop them? Right.

At the base of the low ridgeline, six targets were waiting. They started firing, registering hits on the Klethos who never stopped their charge. At 30 meters out, the Klethos started dropping their disrupter rifles and reaching for the swords slung across their backs.

"Hell, no!" Sergeant Mbangwa shouted.

The light played off the polished blades as they slashed through the air, decapitating or slicing bodies in two, bodies that cost the UAM over 120,000 credits each. As the last automaton fell to the dirt, the eight Klethos stopped, neck frills extended, while they screeched their victory cry.

"Sergeant Blue!" Sergeant Mbangwa shouted over his externals. "I told you to wait for my orders."

He ran to the Klethos he'd designated as "Sergeant Blue" for the exercise, almost chest-bumping the warrior.

"Why did you charge off like that?"

"We won, Sergeant Mbangwa," the Klethos said in her normal voice, which to Hondo, sounded like a mother explaining the obvious to a child.

"Of course, you won, you idiot. Those were training aids, not a real enemy."

A Marine in a PICS massed 800 kg; the Klethos had another 400 kg on top of that, and that sword was both sharp enough and tough enough to cut through a PICS armor, but Sergeant Mbangwa seemed unconcerned that with one flash of Klethos temper, he'd be cut in two.

"We won," the Klethos said again.

"God help me," the sergeant passed on the squad circuit before taking two deep breaths, then saying, "Look, Sergeant Blue. We are trying to learn how to work together. We are trying to teach you Klethos tactics. Melees went out more than a millennium ago."

"A warrior defeats the enemy by force of will," the Klethos said, and for the first time since the battalion had been integrated, Hondo thought he detected a note of what had to be scorn in the Klethos voice.

"If all it took were force of will, then the Grubs wouldn't be kicking your ass all around the galaxy."

Each of the Klethos heard the accusation, and Hondo instinctively tensed for a fight, but they each stood passively while Sergeant Mbangwa lit into them.

"Let me try this, Sergeant," Mbangwa said. "The Klethos-lee came to us for help not because we are bigger or stronger than you are. You came to us because you are losing the war, and you want new ways to fight. You put your honor in the ring with Sally Mae and the Purple Sledgehammer . . ."

At the word "honor," each of the gathered Klethos' neck crest twitched.

". . . to ask for our help. And as honored opponents for 120 years, we agreed. We agreed to become blood brothers and sisters to defend your honor. And now that you are rejecting our help, you give us dishonor."

Oh, nice tack, Sergeant, Hondo acknowledged.

A change came over the Klethos, a slight shift in posture. One of the other warriors said something in their whistling language, and two more responded back in kind. Hondo kept an eye on their crests, knowing if they raised, that a fight was probably in the making.

It wouldn't be the first fight. Two Brotherhood hosts had been killed in what the Klethos explained was a "friendly" fight over honor. That had almost killed the experiment of a mixed Klethos-Human unit, which due to the losses suffered by 3/6 and the survivors' 100% vote to remain with the brigade, had fallen to the battalion.

The twelve remaining Marines and Doc Pataki slowly shifted positions to protect their squad leader if it came to blows.

"This is a matter of honor?" Sergeant Blue asked.

"Yes, it is."

Hondo took a step closer to his sergeant. He didn't know what the Klethos would do when honor was at stake.

Sergeant Blue turned to the other seven Klethos. Whistling and clicking filled the air. Hondo thought he felt the tension in their tone, but as they'd been briefed ad nauseum before the Klethos joined the battalion, he couldn't assign human characteristics to the alien race. "Anthropomorphism," the scientists called it.

The big warrior spun back to Sergeant Mbangwa and fell to her knees, all four arms outstretched, her neck exposed.

"I am shamed I took your honor. I offer myself to you."

The Marines and Doc stepped back, looking at each other in confusion.

"What is the correct way to restore honor to where it belongs?" Sergeant Mbangwa asked in a firm but calm voice.

"Honor is restored when you restore it."

"And if I kill you?"

Shit, sergeant. Don't push it.

"Honor is restored when you restore it," she repeated.

Sergeant Mbangwa slowly placed his PICS foot on the Klethos' neck. The Klethos-lee were large and powerful, but a good stomp in a PICS would break it. Hondo looked at the other Klethos, but he couldn't make out any change of expression or posture. Their neck crests hung limp.

"I say honor is restored," the sergeant said, lifting his foot.

There was the slightest twitch in the Klethos' left minor hand, the only indication that she might have been stressed. She rose and stood silently as if nothing had just happened.

"So, if we can go back to the start, can we do this envelopment again? No melee?"

"As you suggest, Sergeant Mbangwa," Sergeant Blue said.

"Holy shit," BK passed over the fire team net as they all marched back to the range starting line. "I thought we were about to rumble, but Sergeant Mbangwa . . . holy shit!"

"That was pretty intense," Corporal Yetter said.

"Does everybody have balls those big on Paradhiso?" Sam asked Hondo.

"If they do, then what happened to yours, Hondo?" BK asked to the laughter of the other two.

"Eat me," he replied with a smile they couldn't see.

He and the sergeant came from different strata on their home planet, but still, he felt the warm glow of pride. Sergeant Mbangwa was one hell of a Marine.

Chapter 7
Skylar

"That's total bullshit, Sky, and you know it," Knight said, kicking back from the table. "I mean, it just makes no fucking sense."

Sky took three deep breaths, afraid of blowing up at the arrogant asshole. Doctor Knight Hastert was a preeminent organic chemist, something he was never hesitant to remind people. The worst thing about the man was that he was, in fact, brilliant, maybe even to the degree his ego led him to believe.

That doesn't mean he's right here.

"The lack of a nervous system does not automatically mean that the Dictymorphs are colony creatures," she said. "We've got to look beyond the obvious."

"Then why their name. Think of it. And have we ever run across advanced life without a nervous system of some sort?" Knight asked as if that should end the argument.

"Dictymorph" was the accepted term for the enemy, "Dicty" for Dictyostelida, the slime mold that lived independently until a chemical reaction caused them to gather into a singular supermold, and "morph" because they could change their shape. Skylar thought it an unfortunate term. The creatures were far, far advanced beyond the primitive slime molds. The name implied a more basic organism, and that was a dangerous mindset when trying to understand an enemy.

"Knight, we need to consider all possibilities," Peyton said. "Please listen to what Skylar has to offer. She has quite an impressive mind behind her pretty looks."

Oh, God help me! she thought, trying not to roll her eyes in frustration.

Hastert resented her presence on the team, but Janus was trying to get into her panties. Between the two of them, she didn't know what was worse.

Focus on the mission!

The Dictymorph samples had revealed a treasure trove of data, but they were so different from known science that they created more questions than they answered.

Humanity had long thought that science had uncovered most of the universal truths. Sure, there were unanswered questions, but those were only tiny gaps in the total picture. Science had unlocked the secrets of existence.

Humanity had also "known" that the Earth was flat, too, and that rocks didn't float because they "wanted" to move to the center of the universe. And now, with the Dictymorphs, science was having its current Earth-is-not-flat moment.

Even the residue taken from her arm and from other victims defied analysis. It had properties of an acid, but there was more involved in there, something the best AIs were still trying to decipher. There had been molecular damage, whether to armor or tissue, and that caused the initial injury or breach. Beyond that, something kept wounds from healing properly. Sky had gone through the three days of regen the doctors had said she needed, and her wounds had closed, but her arm remained scarred despite the medical team's best efforts.

Luckily, she had been touched by only a tiny amount of splatter. The weapon could take out a PICS, and she shuttered to think of what a full hit would have done to her.

"OK, Sky," Knight continued in the smarmy, condescending tone that made her want to . . . well, she wasn't about to hit the man, but she wanted to do something to him. "Give me five points of analysis that leads to you to conclude that the Dictymorphs are single sentient agencies."

"I don't have five," she admitted. "Sentient, well, I think we've already established that. But for the rest, I just don't think we know enough to arbitrarily dismiss the possibility."

"Arbitrarily? You are accusing me of being arbitrary?" Knight said, looking around at the others with a condescending do-you-hear-this-naive-young-thing-in-over-her-head expression on his face.

OK, maybe I do want to hit him.

"Yes, I am. I think, *Doctor* Hastert, that you are so stuck in your past research that you lack the ability to push beyond that. You lack the ability to delve into the unknown, and that, given our situation, is dangerous," she said, rising to her feet, her eyes glaring.

Knight Hastert's mouth dropped open in surprise, and it took a moment before his face flushed red, surprise being replaced with anger. He sputtered as he rose as well, nothing intelligible coming out.

Finally, he managed a "How dare you, you little unimportant, jumped-up piece of nothing. I've done more 'pushing' into the unknown than you—"

"Doctor Hastert," Executive Counsellor Baker, who was heading the meeting, interrupted. "Sit down. You, too, Doctor Ybarra. Both of you, this is not how men and women of your accomplishments act. I'm surprised at you, acting like children.

"In case either of you haven't noticed, we are at war, and we, those of us in this room, are the real tips of the spears, if I can co-op the Marines' phrasing. We are the tip, because until we can figure out the Dictymorphs, we cannot devise weapons to defeat them, and unless we get those weapons into the hands of the Marines, Host, Legion, and whomever, the Dictymorphs will work their way through Klethos space and into human space."

Sky continued to glare at Knight, leaning forward, hands on the desk in her most aggressive posture. He glared back. But the Executive Counsellor was right. This was bigger than a simple clash of egos, of course. This could be life or death for humanity.

She didn't think she was letting her ego get in the way of rational thinking. She knew she could sometimes carry a chip on her shoulder, she could sometimes be defensive, but she was sure Hastert was blinded to the possibilities.

She took her three deep yoga breaths, and putting the mission first, said, "I am sorry, Knight, if I insulted you. That was not my intent. Of course, I admire your contributions to chemistry."

Hastert glared at her for a few more moments, then said, "I accept your apology."

Oh, you piece of shit, Sky fumed. *That's how you're going to play it? You're not going to offer an apology, too?*

She wanted to scream at him, taking back what she'd said, but she could feel the executive counsellor's eyes bore into her. With an extreme effort of will, she sat back down and remained silent.

Across the table, Janus winked at her.

God save me from these idiots, she prayed as Executive Counsellor Baker got the session back on track.

Chapter 8
Hondo

"Hondo, keep an eye on Mr. Perkins," Corporal Yetter passed.

He gave a quick glance to the left, but Mr. Perkins, named for the berserker serial killer in "Death Comes A'Knocking," was dutifully in his position as the Klethos rifleman.

If anyone were going to break, it would be her. After six weeks of training, most of the Klethos finally seemed to realize that they couldn't simply rush off in a mass assault. The Grubs were simply too powerful for that. If the Klethos-Human military alliance were going to succeed, then they would have to rely on tactics to defeat them.

Hondo wasn't completely sure that the Klethos fighters bought into human tactics, only that the d'solle had determined they would try out the concept. The decision made, honor required that the warriors comply.

Much progress had been made, he had to admit. "Their" squad, except for Mr. Perkins, was reasonably disciplined, and she hadn't broken into an outright melee mode for three days. Still, this dog-and-pony had all the higher-ups in attendance, and the exercise was being live-streamed to every government of man. The stress was bad enough down in the trenches, but the brass must be about shitting bricks, just waiting for the exercise to break down in chaos.

Lieutenant Silas had pulled Hondo and Lyle Masterson from Second Squad, assigning them to bird-dog Mr. Perkins and Boudica, their two biggest liabilities. If either of them so much as twitched wrong, the two Marines were to tackle the Klethos and hold them down. Staff Sergeant Aster, Sergeant Mbangwa, and Corporal Yetter were continually on his butt reminding him to watch Mr. Perkins.

The mission was essentially Infantry Tactics 101, but it was the first time the battalion had operated together since the battle with the Grubs—and it was a far different battalion now. The personnel had been rearranged, other Marines had transferred in, and more importantly, the Klethos were integrated into the unit. Third Squad had been transferred to Mike Company with the eight Klethos taking their place.

Kilo Company was the Point of Main Effort with the mission to assault the automatons making up the enemy. Hondo didn't like the automatons that much. He preferred force-on-force as more dynamic training, but after a few unfortunate incidents with Legionnaires providing the aggressors, that idea had been quickly scrapped. The task force couldn't afford to lose any of their fighting strength in training.

With Mike providing the base of fire and Lima positioned in support, the mission was one the Marines could do sleepwalking. Marines and Klethos, however, did not yet instill the same feeling of confidence.

Kilo kept up the advance. Demo-pyro exploded around them. The Marines were used to them, and the Klethos didn't seem fazed even when pelted with clods of dirt shot into the air.

"Makes no damned sense, this pyro," BK passed. "We need Grub light weapons, not this shit."

"We'll have them. Did you see them uncrate the Grubs?" Sam responded.

Hondo wasn't so sure they would see the huge automatons anytime soon. At half-a-billion credits each, the huge, realistic-looking replicas made by DreamWorks were too valuable to risk to crazed Klethos. They could even "kill" Marines in PICS, the light weapons tuned to sensors that could be activated in the combat suits. Hondo thought they'd be held in limbo until human-only follow-on forces arrived for training.

"Second Platoon, hold up. We're getting ahead of the rest of the company," the lieutenant passed.

Hondo checked his order of battle display. If they had edged out past the other platoons, it wasn't by much. The lieutenant was relatively laid back as far as officers go, but if she was on them like this, she must be getting the same kind of pressure from above.

The Klethos weren't used to having someone else control their movement, but this time, all eight complied. They stood still like good little soldiers until the command was given to move out again.

At 800 meters, the company came online. Mike took the enemy under fire, and Kilo steadily advanced at the half-trot, eating up the ground. PICS registered hits from enemy fire, but no one faltered. No one did much about the incoming, either. This was not a realistic scenario by any means. It was merely a "proof of concept," the battalion commander had told them during the brief.

With only the last slope between the enemy and them, Kilo charged the position, knocking out each of the enemy. The Klethos kept under control, with not a single sword drawn. Probably best of all for the maintenance crews, not a single automaton was damaged.

Kilo consolidated on the far side of the objective, providing security for Lima to advance. Once Lima arrived, the exercise was brought to endex, probably to the great relief of the task force. The combined Marine-Klethos unit had performed without any major screw-ups.

Hondo didn't feel a sense of accomplishment as the NCOs and above congratulated each other on a job well done. This was a BS operation, but above and beyond that, it just didn't feel right. The Klethos didn't seem into it. They were going through the motions, nothing more. There was none of that crazed sense of purpose that had taken Sergeant Blue and his squad into a rampage of destroying automatons.

The entire premise of the Klethos-Human task force was that humans would bring tactical expertise while the Klethos shoulder the bulk of the fight. He just didn't see that fight in the Klethos today. True, the Marines were mostly going through the motions as well, but things just didn't sit right with him.

"Hey, uh . . . did the Klethos . . . I mean, did they seem a little lethargic to you guys today?" he asked on the fire team net.

"What, them? Yeah, like someone took their balls," BK said.

"They're female, BK, not male. No balls," Sam said, laughing.

"No matter. Everybody's got balls. Yours just dangle."

"I mean it. Look at them. They're pretty relaxed."

"Don't worry about it none," BK said. "We told them not to go all berserker today, or their honor and shit would be lost. They just obeyed orders for once."

"Maybe," Hondo replied without conviction.

I just hope we're doing this right.

Chapter 9
Skylar

"That went well," Peyton said, moving to intercept her as she left the stands.

The head xenobiologist was still a pain in the neck with his attention, but he'd become one of her few allies, and if working with the devil got her views heard, that was a sacrifice she was willing to make.

He was right, though. It had gone fairly well. The Marines and the Klethos had managed to conduct an assault without screwing up. With this checkmark done, the next step would be to conduct operations with the other units in the task force.

With all the focus on the Dictymorphs, Sky had almost forgotten that her field of expertise was the Klethos-lee. Watching the exercise, she tried to fit in what she'd observed with her previously-held ideas. Not all of it matched.

The military had a team of xeno-scientists attached to them, helping to facilitate the integration, while she, perhaps the most qualified person on the planet, fought with colleagues about the Dictymorphs. What she was doing was vital to the mission, but still, she felt a longing to be jumping into deeper waters with the Klethos.

The introduction of the d'solle leadership class had been a huge surprise, but now, that fact had simply been overcome by events. More and more of the social organization was being revealed, each new piece of information something she would have killed for only a year prior.

The d'relle were already well known, as was the propensity for the Klethos, other than the warriors, to conduct business in quads. Almost everything else was new. Over breakfast, she overheard someone on the Klethos team remarking that one of the head-quad's members was a male.

Ah, the smaller one, she noted, then chastised herself for assuming.

It had been long understood that the Klethos, just as with most Earth-based life, were both male and female. The d'relle were female (which was why Gladiators were female as well), and the warriors were female. Despite all sorts of probes conducted at challenges, no one had been able to identify a Klethos male. With the bird/dinosaur analog, most people assumed that the males were simply smaller versions of the female, and that could be true. As a scientist, however, Sky could not fall into the trap of assumptions.

She wondered what else she was missing, and for a moment, she was tempted to take the afternoon off and ask for an update from the Klethos team.

"You want to walk with me?" Peyton asked, snapping her back to the here and now.

"What?" she asked stupidly.

"Do you want to walk with me? To the conference call?"

Oh, hell. How did I forget that?

"The Jesuits, yes."

"So, yes, do you want to walk with me?" he asked confused.

"Yes, we can walk together. Any indication of what they've found?"

"I would imagine it has to do with sequencing," he said, his eyebrows drawn together in puzzlement.

No shit, Sky. Snap back out of it.

The Saint Peter Canisius Monastery, an independent enclave on the Brotherhood world of Destiny, had grown to be one of the finest experimental laboratories in human space. Specializing in sequencing the very quarks and leptons that made matter, it made sense that was what the conference was to cover. And if the Jesuit brothers felt comfortable enough to reveal their findings, they could be pretty significant.

Thoughts of Klethos pushed aside, she hurried with Peyton to find out what piece of the Dictymorph puzzle might have been found.

K-1003

Chapter 10
Hondo

Hondo's pulse raced with nervous energy as he waited in the assembly area for the order to move out. Twenty-five clicks ahead of them in the darkness was a concentration of Grubs.

The unnamed planet, designated K-1003 by the UAM command, was deep into Klethos space, across a vast arm of the galaxy where up until then, no humans had ventured. The explorer aspect of that was lost on Hondo—he, along with the rest of the humans in the task force, was more concerned with the Grubs that awaited them.

The planet had fallen to the Grubs more than 20 Earth-standard years prior, according to the Klethos. A very small number of the Grubs, possibly fewer than a hundred, remained on the planet for reasons no one knew.

Not that most of what the Grubs did made sense to the humans. While generally pushing in from the the center of the Virgo Supercluster's center, they seemed to hit some planets and not others. The Klethos hadn't been able to determine just what they did with a planet once they took it.

"You ready to joust?" BK asked over the fire team net, nudging his arm with a clank of battle armor.

"Ooh-rah," he answered. "Born ready."

"I'm gonna kick me some Grub ass," she passed.

"They don't have asses," Sam interjected.

"I'll kick your ass, then."

"I know you've wanted my ass for a long time, sister."

Hondo barely listened to the banter of his friends. Some Marines became overly garrulous before a fight, others withdrew into themselves. Hondo tended to get quiet as he went over the operations order in his mind, trying to foresee any change to it.

And it would change. The ancient proverb that no battle plan lasts beyond the first contact was just as valid today as it was back on Earth with the land armies.

More chance for it all go haywire on this mission, he noted to himself as he gripped the pike in his left gauntlet.

One-third of the Marines had been issued the Klethos pikes, the same ones with which they'd killed one of the Grubs in the last battle. Three meters long, with 80 cm of that the point, they crackled with occasional snaps and pops as the frequency of the current alternated. The human research team couldn't agree whether it was the sharp point and edge or the current that had taken down the Grub. All Hondo knew was that the Grub had killed most of the Klethos wielding them, and that didn't give him a warm and fuzzy. If it came down to it, he'd trust his M-48 more. He knew the higher-ups wanted to find out what weapons worked the best, and he understood that, but when it got down to brass tacks, he had to protect his mother's favorite Marine.

BK's comment about jousting had become a running joke within the battalion. With the long lance-like pikes, the PICS Marines did somewhat look like knights of the Middles Ages. Give them giant destriers, and they'd fit right in, Saint George galloping off to slay the dragon—if a giant white grub could be considered as one.

Those Marines who hadn't been issued a pike had a variety of weapons, all gyvered to see what might have an effect. The Klethos in the battalion kept their own weapons.

This time, 3/6 was not the lead element, nor even in the main assault wave. That honor went to a Brotherhood and a Confederation battalion along with a French company and two Klethos "battalions" (the Klethos did not seem to have units as the humans considered them. Each group and a commander and some sub-commanders, but after that, there wasn't any organization that they could discern).

More than a few of the 3/6 Marines, still angry over the last battle, wanted to be the tip of the spear in order to deal out revenge. Revenge was all well and good, but not when it colored your actions. The real reason they were in the reserve, though, was that as the mixed battalion, no one knew if they were ready for combat ops yet.

Glancing over at Third Squad (K), Hondo wasn't sure, either. The eight Klethos stood easy with no sign of nerves. The Klethos as a whole seemed to have accepted the need for unit integrity, but Hondo wasn't sure they'd embraced human tactics. Mr. Perkins, in particular, seemed to be just going through the motions.

At least Sergeant Blue seems to be acting like an NCO.

It was true. Over the last four months, the Klethos had essentially eased into a real leadership role, and the other Klethos took seemed to accept her leadership. Sam thought it was simply a case of the billet defining the individual. She'd been named "Sergeant" and had grown into the position.

"We're moving out in five," Staff Sergeant Aster passed. "Get yourselves ready."

Hondo checked his readouts for the twentieth time. He had his combat load of six M-48s, ten thousand rounds of flechettes, twenty 20mm grenades . . . and a Klethos pike. His power was at 97%. He was ready for bear (or Grubs, he hoped).

Five klicks ahead, the Brotherhood, Confed, and the two Klethos battalions and the Greater French company were moving out, all to face about 20 Grubs. Twenty-five hundred humans and a thousand Klethos.

Four Falcon-Cs were staged 90 klicks away, but after what happened to the first two and the *CS Philippi,* they were only to be called forward as a last-ditch option.

"We're expendable, not them," Sam had noted.

Hondo didn't think that was true . . . not exactly. No one knew what the Grubs had used to knock down the *Philippi,* even after months of analysis, while they had a better idea of what they used on the Marines and Klethos. They couldn't replicate it, and armor only gave very temporary protection, but the infantry could take the fight to the enemy.

He was just glad he wasn't in the French Legion. In their Rigaudeau-6's, which the Marines had to grudgingly admit were superior to their PICS, the Legionnaires had been outfitted with several types of armor shields, each shield crammed with analytic devices. Their mission was to get hit by the Grubs and then see how well the various shields protected them.

Max balls, as BK would say.

"Move out," the lieutenant passed on the command net.

"Let's go, Sergeant Blue," Staff Sergeant Aster passed to the Klethos in the platoon, stepping up and giving the hand-and-arm signal to move.

The Klethos didn't seem to like comms, and only Blue and Beanie had headsets, which they'd turn off as often as not. Sergeant Blue raised an upper fist in acknowledgment, however, and the platoon started forward.

Hondo kept his pike head out in front of him, careful not to let it drift too close to his body. When humans and Klethos had first clashed, the Klethos had been able to render most of the Marine and New Budapest weapons inoperable through a projected field. The pike head worked on a similar basis, supposedly interfering with the Grubs' bodies, but if it got too close to a human weapons system, it could knock that out, too.

With night vision and full magnification, Hondo could see the rear elements of the Brotherhood battalion ahead of him. They were moving steadily forward, using a network of ancient washes for cover. This region of K-1003 was barren of life, just rocks and sand that could easily be mistaken for the Wicked Dry, the largest desert on Paradhiso. Most of the host was out of sight already with only the artillery battery visible. Three-Six was to advance to the battery and provide security while the other units advanced into contact. Along with 2/14, the two Marine battalions were the totality of the task force reserve. General Reicker had wanted the entire Marine brigade, but the task force lacked the stealth transport from space to the ground to land that many bodies.

It took only 15 minutes to move into position. The Brotherhood battery had eight Cana and eight Eden tubes, the Eden firing the smart 190mm shells, and Hondo looked at them with interest. It was commonly accepted that the Eden AP shells were designed as PICS killers despite the fact that the Federation and the Brotherhood had never been openly at war. This was the closest Hondo had ever been to one of the big guns.

The Confed had some of their big meson canons to employ, but they'd be deployed in the envelopment, not here in support of the fixing force. Hondo had seen his own M-48 missiles simply be absorbed by the Grubs, so despite the big shells being fired by the battery, he'd put his money on the meson canons.

Sergeant Mbangwa loomed out of the darkness, checking positions of the three squads. As he reached Hondo, he switched to the P2P and said, "Keep an eye on the Klethos, OK? I'm going to want to give the lieutenant a full report when all this is over."

"Roger that, Sergeant," Hondo replied. "I've got it."

"Good man, Soldier" the sergeant passed, giving him a swipe on the back that would have torn a man out of armor in two.

Hondo felt a surge of pride. Since he was a child, he'd been taught to respect the Youmambo class. As on all Federation worlds now, citizens were equal, but sometimes, one class is more equal than another. Three hundred years of the Youmambo ruling the planet could not be poofed away like dust in the wind. Sergeant Mbangwa was a Youmanbo, a "Black Blood," and just like a fan meeting a celebrity, Hondo still felt a thrill when the sergeant singled him out.

He knew that feeling was misplaced. They both were Marines, and the Corps didn't care about Black Bloods or anything else. Mbangwa was his senior by his rank of sergeant, nothing else.

Still, Hondo was a creature of his upbringing, and he could help but feel a bit of pride that the sergeant was leaning on him.

He kept his scanners at maximum reach, not that he thought he'd need them if a Grub came by, but he kept watch on the four Klethos in his sight. They looked calm and in control, but who knew what might spark them into charging off in a fury?

"The Confed are in contact," the company commander passed. "Stay ready for orders."

"The skipper must be getting nervous," BK passed with a laugh. "He never gets on the net."

Which was true. Captain Montgomery did not micromanage. He let his subordinate leaders lead. He probably was on the command net to the lieutenant, but he rarely reached down to the grunt level.

More than 20 klicks in the distance, the skyline lit up. Hondo wished he could see what was going on, but just as the skipper didn't go down to their level, neither did the flow of information. If the fighting became a threat to them, they would hear it, but until then, they could only imagine what was happening.

There was a whoosh of air as the battery opened fire with its Eden guns. The magnetic rings around the tubes accelerated the rounds, giving them a range of at least 60km (the Brotherhood Host kept the exact range a secret). Hondo counted 32 rounds going downrange.

"Standby for counter-battery fire," one of the Brotherhood soldiers announced on the AOR open net.

Hondo and BK exchanged glances. The rounds wouldn't even have landed yet, and if the Grubs had artillery of some sort, they hadn't yet shown any sign of it.

"Maybe that's just the Brothers' SOP," Hondo told her.

"Maybe," BK said. "Shit, how long have we been supposedly cross-training? And we don't have a friggin' universal SOP?"

"Well, we've been busy with the Klucks," Hondo said. "Not much time to work with the other humans."

"Don't let the staff sergeant hear you say Klucks," she warned.

"That's why I'm on the P2P, BK. I'm not that stupid."

The term had begun to be put in use for a couple of months now. Some of the sounds made in the Klethos language could be taken for a chicken cluck, but the real reason was more likely that it rhymed with a certain word popular with soldiers for millennia. The brass was not amused, although when asked, their Klethos squad took no issue with the term.

"Still, I'm surprised at you, Mr. Straight-and-Narrow, letting your mouth come down in the gutter with us dirty peons."

"Yeah, right. It's not a bad word."

"Cut the chatter," Corporal Yetter said on the fire team net.

For a moment, Hondo thought he'd been listening in, but then he realized that for all intents and purposes, the P2Ps were secure, but their use was not. Yetter could see that they were chatting, even if he didn't know about what.

"Yeah, McKeever. Cut the chatter," BK said, assigning him the blame.

Hondo gave her an armored middle finger, then turned to look back towards the fight. Confederation soldiers were engaged in the distance, yet here they were BS'ing around. The sound of muffled explosions reached him, probably the first of the Eden rounds to reach the enemy.

As Hondo watched, two lights, almost like old-fashioned flares, reached up in the distance. Instead of arching back down, they continued, higher and higher, heading in their direction.

"Corporal Yetter, do you—" he started before his fire team leader cut him off.

"Yes, we see it. Wait for orders,"

In other words, shut up and let them figure out what to do.

"What the fuck's that?" Sam asked as the two lights closed the distance.

"I wish I knew," Hondo said, an empty feeling in the pit of his stomach as the lights came closer.

"Engage the lights," the order came down as two avatars representing the lights appeared on his display. Range was six klicks and closing.

Hondo didn't hesitate. His first M-48 was off within four seconds, his second cycling to his launcher to fire. All around him, Marine and Brotherhood weapons reached up to the lights, tracers and exhaust trails lighting up the sky. Hondo fired again just as his first hit—that is, just as his first passed through the light. The missile didn't detonate. From the arming selection Hondo had given it, passing within ten meters of anything over five kilos would have triggered the warhead. He was sure he hadn't missed. He checked his targeting AI and confirmed the missile had passed directly through the center of the sphere of light.

His second missile failed to detonate as well. Explosions filled the sky as the Cana tubes put out curtains of flak, but the two spheres kept advancing.

A crackle of energy went over Hondo's head, and he spun to see two of the Klethos firing their bell-muzzled "ray guns," one of the projectors that could shut down any Marine weapon. The other six Klethos stood silently and watched. Hondo spun back to see one of the lights seem to falter before picking back up to speed.

"This isn't good," Sam said in an understatement as the lights raced towards them.

Just as the spheres reached to the front edge of the battery's position, tendrils of Tesla-like light shot out of them, all aimed at the ground. Twenty meters to his right, the nearest tube took a direct hit. Secondary tendrils bounced off the tube, hitting the two-man crew, dropping them to the dirt. A flash of light blinded him for a moment, overcoming his display, before the compensators brought his vision back to normal.

Now significantly smaller, the spheres kept advancing, 100 meters above the ground. Another crack of Klethos energy reached out and hit one of the spheres, and this time, it flickered and went out. The second sphere unleashed another barrage of light fingers. The sphere shrunk as its light weapons splayed across the ground until there was nothing left, and it simply went out.

Most of the outgoing fire had ceased, but rounds were still going out until a "Cease fire, cease fire," echoed throughout the net.

Hondo stood in shock.

What the hell was that?

He started forward to the nearest tube, but while there hadn't been any explosions, there was no doubt it had been hit. The tube was out of action, slumped and half-melted. The two Brotherhood gun-crew were both dramatically KIA, probably with too much damage for resurrection. Beyond that gun, Hondo could see that the next gun was down as well, a gaping hole in the breach.

Hondo wheeled and started running to the Klethos, who were simply standing as if nothing much had just happened.

"Hondo—" BK started, but he ran right past her.

"Sergeant Blue," he asked the big Klethos warrior. "What was that?"

"That was a Grub," she said as if explaining the obvious.

"No, I mean what kind of weapon?"

"Weapon? That was the Grub."

"Not who shot it. What was it? I hit it with my M-48, and nothing happened."

Sergeant Blue turned to the others and started a conversation. Staff Sergeant Aster was already consolidating the forces before the Klethos turned back to Hondo.

"The weapon is the Grub. Like a pimple," she said, as if unfamiliar with the word. "The Grub sent the pimple out with its life, then spent that force on you humans. Boudica was able to deplete one after the first discharge weakened it."

"Soldier, get your ass back here," Sergeant Mbangwa passed to Hondo on the P2P. "And bring the Klucks with you."

Hondo knew the Klethos had just said something significant, but he couldn't figure out what. He hit the save on his conversation, then brought the Klethos squad with him as he joined the rest of the squad at the first destroyed tube.

Close up, it looked more like the ancient artist Dali had painted it. The gun slumped, as if the most of the very molecules holding it together had simply lost their grip.

Most of the Brotherhood soldiers, in their personal body armor, were dead, as were the Klethos attached to First Platoon. The Marines in their PICS and two squads of Klethos, those who'd been farthest away, were unhurt, although many of the PICS had been drained. To his surprise, Hondo's PICS was now at 62%. The flash that had blinded him had evidently been a tendril of the weapon.

"OK, this is where we're at," Sergeant Mbangwa said. "The Brotherhood battery is gone. Doc Tolstoy is working on a handful of the soldiers, but it's icicle time and hope they get zombie when we get them back to the real world."

Hondo was surprised that any of them had a chance, but he hadn't seen those on the far side of the battery. Maybe the carnage was less there.

"Staff Sergeant Jardine's coming around right after she checks Third Platoon, so we stay here until she gives each PICS the once-over."

The staff sergeant was CWO4 Donaldson's assistant armorer and had been attached to the company headquarters for the mission.

"We're on deck, so don't anyone of you wander off. Once each fire team gets an up-check, go back to the perimeter and wait."

"It's always waiting," BK passed on the fire team net.

"You want to go up there now?" Sam asked, pointing to the light show in the distance.

"Sergeant Blue, are your people OK?"

Hondo had forgotten that the Klethos were not monitored by the Marine battle AI. If any one of them were hurt, Sergeant Mbangwa wouldn't know.

"We are all able to fight," the Klethos warrior said.

Hondo looked over them. Two seemed worse for wear, but they weren't complaining.

"I would've thought the Klucks would have run amok when we got hit, but they kinda just stood there. Only two of them fired their blunderbusses," BK said.

Hondo agreed. Out there, he had to think two Klethos battalions were getting pummeled, but their eight seemed to be calm and collected.

It took Staff Sergeant Jardine fifteen minutes to reach them, all the time, the signs of battle lighting up the sky. Hondo ached to know what was going on. Nobody kept the non-rates informed, though. The staff sergeant gave Hondo the OK, reminding him that he was down to 62%.

As soon as the corporal was given the up-check, the four Marines went back to their position, facing outboard. They each had sectors to watch, and the sergeant had asked him to keep an eye on the Klethos, but his gaze kept straying to the light show. He wished someone would let them know what was going on.

"Hey, Sam. How about you and me go up there and show the Grubs what's what?" BK passed.

"Nah, take Hondo. The fire team needs me here, right Corporal?"

"Yeah, right, Sam," Yetter said. "And I even think the colonel would want you back in the rear with the gear with him."

"Sounds good to me. Hot chow, showers. My kind of place."

The banter interjected a feeling of normalcy to the team, which was amazing considering their situation. On a planet where no humans had been, alongside humanity's enemy of the last century, and facing huge deadly caterpillars, nothing should have been ordinary.

Just a normal mission, McKeever. Nothing more.

Of course, the gods of war chose that moment to throw in a monkey wrench.

"Kilo Company, we have a new mission," Captain Montgomery passed on the net. "All forces are pulling back for retrograde. We're moving forward to provide flank security."

"What, did they win already?" BK asked on the fire team net.

"Not if we're there for security," Hondo told her.

Their face shield displays lit up with streams of data laying out their new positions. Second Platoon was to take the relatively high ground ten klicks forward, becoming part of the west side of the security corridor. A PICS platoon could cover an 800-meter frontage. With one of their squads now Klethos, that had dropped to about 600 meters during training on Purgamentium. Now, though, their frontage was a full 1300 meters.

Either the threat is low, or things have gone to shit, and we've got to make due.

Given the mere fact that they were being given the mission, Hondo was betting on the latter.

Within moments, they were moving out in a battalion V, Kilo and Lima leading on opposite fingers of high ground, India at the V's base and in the low ground with Mike hanging back. This gave them more firepower to the front and allowed quicker movement. Each platoon would drop off at its position as the battalion moved.

With the battalion in a V, Captain Montgomery had put the company in a wedge, Second Platoon on the highest ground, First and Third along the slopes. Hondo felt exposed as he jogged, his sensors reaching out for signs of danger. His PICS had fairly decent night vision, but it was limited to about 200 meters. Much farther than that, he has to rely on active pinging.

"How are the Klucks doing, Soldier?" Sergeant Mbangwa asked him on the P2P. "They keeping up?"

He looked back to his right, and he spotted six of the eight, all jogging along.

"Roger that, Sergeant. No problem. Still calm."

"Let me know if they start falling back," he passed, then added, "Or if they start pushing ahead."

The Klethos had seemed to accept the need for unit integrity, but that was in training. Who knew if that discipline would hold?

They crested a low rise covered with boulders and had just started down the other slope when lights filled the air, causing his face shield to flare out for a moment before the compensators could take ahold.

"Contact left!" several Marines shouted at once over the net.

The fire team, with untold hours of immediate action drills, pivoted as one to face the threat. Fingers of light reached out, splashing Marines in Second Squad. One of them was highlighted in a corona of blue light not 100 meters from Hondo before collapsing in a heap.

"Move it," Sergeant Mbangwa shouted, leading the charge.

The platoon had been ambushed by a Grub the size of a rhino, and most of Kilo was in the kill zone. Remaining in a kill zone invited death. Marines had a tried and true method of getting out of a kill zone: charge the ambushers.

Or, in this case, the ambusher, singular. Despite the size of the thing, Hondo couldn't see it through the boulders.

Its location was pretty clear, though, given the light show, and First Squad rushed to support Second.

"Check your Charlie telltales!" the company gunny passed over the net.

Hondo gave his display a quick look—the Charlie telltale's light was a steady green. Sergeant Killkillary, the FO from Weapons Company, was about to call for fire from the mortarbots. The MM-30 Automated Battalion Mortar System was fairly new to the battalion, supposedly offering much more firepower and accuracy than the old mortars, but it required a separate telltale to keep the rounds from hitting, and taking out, PICS Marines.

He pushed that out of his mind as he ran forward, tendrils of light passing over his head as they sought out Marines. He still didn't have a target. The Grub had picked a well-protected spot where it had good cover. The Marines were going to have to pry it out.

A series of explosions burst in the air in front of the charging Marines, the mortar rounds directing 2cm-wide, 90 cm-long steel bars at the Grub. The lights stopped for a moment, and Hondo felt a surge of excitement before several spheres of light shot up into the air. He'd just seen these, and he knew his M-48s had no effect, but he fired again, hoping that the close range might make a difference.

It didn't. His missile flew through the light without detonating. His instinct was to take cover, but the spheres of light passed over his head.

"They're going for the mortarbots," BK said.

The MM-30's were new pieces of gear, meant to eliminate the need for a Marine-manned mortar section, but they weren't entirely trusted. Distrust or not, Hondo fervently hoped the mortarbots could stand up better than the Brotherhood tubes.

"Push forward, First," Sergeant Mbangwa ordered. "Let's see if hitting them can fuck up their command and control of the light spheres."

Hondo stepped around a large boulder, and the Grub was suddenly in sight, forty meters away. This was right about at the edge of the M-48's arming distance, but he fired anyway, the missile impacting an instant later. There was a slight flash of blue light on the thing's side, but nothing else.

"I need something to kill it with!" Hondo shouted.

There was a crack of ionized air and a flash as something hit the Grub from above, and the enemy recoiled. For a moment, Hondo thought one of the ships had come to the rescue, but the blast was too small. It had to be one of the combat drones. Another beam hit the Grub, and he could see the fire was hurting it.

And then, from another 100 meters to the right of the Grub, a concentrated finger of light reached up into the sky.

"Sons-of-bitches, there's another one of them," Corporal Yetter said.

"Damn, glad the drone flushed that guy," Sam said.

Hondo didn't know what would have happened had the second Grub opened up on them in another ambush. The drone might not have scored a kill, but it might have just saved their asses.

"First Squad, shift right," Lieutenant Silas ordered. "Sergeant Blue, move into the gap."

Sergeant Mbangwa acknowledged the order, but the Klethos squad leader was silent.

"Sergeant Blue, acknowledge."

"We are complying," the Klethos finally passed.

"What the hell's wrong with them?" BK asked on the team net. "They better get their asses in gear."

"We need to fix these two in place while Third Platoon envelopes from the right. It's up to Kilo, Marines. Lima is getting hit, too," the lieutenant passed as the specifics popped up on their displays.

Hondo took a moment to look behind him. About a click away, on the other side of the high ground, more lights and explosions lit up the darkness.

"It's a double ambush," Hondo said over the fire team net. "Simple, but it's working."

"Don't worry about double anything. We've got our mission right here," Corporal Yetter told him. "Skirmishers left."

The four Marines slid into the formation, used to maximize firepower front toward a known enemy. Together, they advanced, pouring fire into the Grub. It was probably ineffective, but as the lieutenant had said when giving them the op order, it was possible that cumulative fire could get the job done when a single volley wasn't enough.

Hondo cycled one of his volcs to his launcher. The MI-222 was a slow-burning incendiary grenade intended for destruction of equipment on the battlefield, but it could be launched out to about 40 meters as well. Given the evident shielding on the thing, he doubted the grenade would have much effect, but it wasn't doing him much good inside his magazine.

With a thunk, the grenade arched upwards, its mechanical fuze already rotating. Hondo had already cycled in his 40mm when the volc hit the Grub right on top. It erupted into a tiny, bright star, and the Grub convulsed, its light tendrils momentarily stopping while is shook like a bronco.

Hondo felt a moment of astounded victory until with a huge flick that rumbled down the length of the Grub's body in a wave, the still-burning volc was flung off and to the ground.

"BK, max thermo," Corporal Yetter ordered.

He'd seen Hondo's volc. BK, with her meson cannon, could adjust the frequency and focus of the beam to create heat when it struck something solid. In an instant, she could hit the Grub with the same amount of heat as a volc took over a minute to expend.

"Got it, boss," she answered. A moment later, she said, "Nothing. It didn't even flinch, damn it."

A tendril of light reached out and hit her. She dodged to the right into cover. The tendril drifted, as if seeking her out.

A bulge lifted from the top of the Grub, elongating into a fleshy mound. Hondo joined six or seven Marines on firing at the mound just as the tip of it separated into two of the light spheres. Rounds ricocheted off as they hit, but several grenades seemed to penetrate into its body. A chunk of Grub-flesh broke off, and the creature seemed to contract upon itself, its skin smoothing out.

"We're hurting it!" Sergeant Mbangwa shouted. "Keep up the pressure."

With the eight Klethos from Third Squad and seven more from First Platoon's Third Squad closing in on the second Grub, that left First and Second Squad facing the first one. As the Marines closed in, the Grub seemed to focus more on them. Light reached out, and within moments, three Marines were down. Hondo could see their avatars on his display flash to gray, but he couldn't take the time to see who they were.

More volcs were hitting the Grub, and it was definitely not happy. The light tendrils increase in number, and one tendril splayed across Hondo's chest. His alarm screamed out a warning, and Hondo was about to boost-jump when he broke in the clear.

The red flashing 18% let him know his power was below combat-ready minimums. There was no retreating to the rear to get recharged, though.

"Beamers, focus on the the right front," the lieutenant passed, spotting where she wanted them to target. "Everyone else, expend your volcs, then use your pikes!"

The platoon had practiced the pike drill a hundred times or more back on Purgamentium, both with all hands and with one or more PICS deploying other weapons. Hondo shifted his pike to his right arm, not that it made any difference in his PICS, and slid to the right, covering BK. He clamped his gauntlet closed—nothing was going to be able to pry the pike loose.

Here it goes!

With three final steps, he plunged the pike into the Grub's side. He expected more resistance, but the sharpened head easily pierced the skin, and he had to stop himself from physically colliding with it.

Brute, on his left, ran his pike all the way to the hilt, and as soon as his hands reached the pulsing white skin, the blue aura-like glow flowed around and encased him.

"Brute! Push back!" Hondo shouted over the net.

Brute struggled a moment before he stopped moving and his avatar switched to gray on Hondo's display.

Hondo reached back to grab the protruding hilt of his pike, intending to drive it in deeper when a flap of Grub shot out of its side, a meter adjacent to where his pike was buried. Three years of training took over as Hondo extended his right arm to fire on the flap . . .

. . . training that put him in mortal danger. The flap narrowed to a tentacle and shot around Hondo's neck. He tried to reverse and pull back, but with tremendous force, the Grub pulled him into its embrace. His suit alarm gave an aborted squeal before his PICS went dead.

Hondo was blind. He hit the emergency power, but nothing happened.

Go through your steps! he told himself in his rising panic.

One: Activate emergency power!

He tried it again, but with the same result.

Two: Pump the primer three times and restart.

Still, his PICS didn't react.

Three: Signal for emergency evac.

He thumbed the button, but there was no indication that the self-powered signal was sent.

Four: Combat molt.

He hesitated at this. He was motionless, the best he could tell, so he might not still be in the Grub's grasp. If he was, however, and he molted, he'd be a dead man. He had to see what was going on.

Without power, there was only one way to do this. He pulled his left arm out of its sleeve, reached up, and by feeling in the dark, found the fiber knob. The knob was mechanically attached to a tiny covered porthole, and each turn opened the periscope cover. Flashes of light flickered across his faceplate display, and for a moment, Hondo thought it was malfunctioning, but as he opened it farther, the image was reflected onto the inner layer of his display. The lights were from the Grub, now four or five meters away from him. Without power, he had no night vision, but the light show was more than enough for him to get his bearings.

A Marine, probably Brute, was motionless beside him, frozen in a lunge. Beyond Brute, another Marine was pouring beamer fire into the Grub at point-blank range.

The scene was surreal. With no sound reaching him except for his heavy breathing, Hondo felt as if he were watching the fight through a telescope. He was very aware of the emergency molt lever by his left thigh, but he couldn't tell if it would be safe for him outside of his PICS, dead as it was.

A tendril of light touched the Marine with the beamer.

Break away.

But the Marine didn't. Dropping the useless weapon, he or she reached for the pike, and then just sort of came apart as the light danced over them. The PICS collapsed, falling into a disjointed heap on the ground. Hondo didn't need a working order of battle display to know that whoever it was had just died.

The tendril lingered a moment, then almost meandered five meters across the ground to where Brute stood frozen in his lunge.

Hondo was still alive, so he'd hoped Brute was too, that they'd both get out of this in one piece. He cried out in agony when the light caught Brute, flaring him that horrible shade of luminescent blue. Four, five seconds later, Brute's PICS collapsed as well, almost flowing as it came apart.

In 15 seconds, Hondo has just seen two Marines killed while he stood by, helpless to save either one. He screamed in frustration, a scream cut off when the light finger started to advance on him.

Two: Pump the primer three times and restart. Two: Pump the primer three times and restart, he told himself as he furiously pushed on the button and hit the start.

Nothing.

At that moment, Hondo knew he was going to die, and a feeling of calm swept over him. He'd have thought he would go down kicking and screaming if it came to that, but no. He watched the light come up to him, then blue light filled his optics.

What's it going to feel like, coming apart?

The shock jolted him.

"What the . . . ?"

He'd hit hard, and now he was on his side. Most of his vision was obscured, but he saw the feet of a PICS advancing on the Grub before they passed through his field of view.

What's going on? he wondered, his mind dazed and not grasping reality.

It took him a moment before he realized that he was still alive. He was on his side, he was in an unpowered suit, but he was alive. He might have been calm as he watched the Grim Reaper come to him, but now that he was alive, his emotions almost overcame him.

I'm fucking alive!

Now, how to keep that way?

He realized that one of his fellow Marines had knocked him out of the Grub's grip, then taken the fight to it. Hondo had been given a reprieve, but that didn't mean he was out of the woods. He had no power, and other than the 2mm Colt-Ruger clipped into the holster attached next to the emergency molt lever, he was unarmed.

Still, I'm alive.

Hondo's vision was extremely limited, and as the Grub moved, the fight shifted out of his vision. All he could do was watch the reflections of light and the few tendrils that flashed across his field of view. After a few minutes, the lights seemed to peter out, becoming fewer and fewer.

The immediate fight might be ending, but Hondo knew that things were going badly for the humans and Klethos; otherwise, the Brotherhood battalion wouldn't be withdrawing. If the survivors hadn't already passed by on the way to the pickup site, they would be soon. Hondo could not afford to let them pass him by.

It had to be now.

Taking a deep breath, he reached for the lever and triggered the molt. Slowly, too slowly, the hydraulics pushed the suit apart along the seams. Air sharp with the tang of ionization blew inside. Hondo grabbed his 2mm and performed the contortion required to back out of his PICS, then jumped to his feet, clad only in his longjohns, the form-fitting suit that a Marine wore while in a PICS.

The Grub was gone, but not so the Marines. Five destroyed PICS were scattered around him. Beside a boulder, another PICS was basically whole, standing normally, its split back evidence that the Marine had molted. There could have been others, but in the darkness, he couldn't see much more than that.

As he moved forward, handgun at the ready, a flare of light reflected off the standing PICS, revealing the small four-leaf clover patched on the back shoulder.

"BK!" Hondo shouted, rushing ahead, mindless of anything else.

He rounded the PICS and skidded to a halt. BK was sitting on the ground, with what looked like a torn doll in her lap.

Oh, shit, shit, shit.

The PICS on the ground was destroyed. Almost one entire side and both legs had the same kind of damage as the other destroyed PICS. The rest looked whole. Hondo didn't have to ask whose PICS that was as he reached BK.

Sam, his legs, pelvis, and one arm simply gone, looked up at him, and said in slurred words, "Glad I didn't waste my effort."

That hit Hondo like a mule kick, and he felt faint.

"You did that? You save me?" he asked, already knowing the answer.

Of course, it would be Sam. Or BK. Or Yetter. They were family.

"Someone had to take care of you," he said before slipping into a series of coughs.

"Shhhhh, Sam. We'll get you back."

"What, so you can keep telling me I owe you one? Fat chance. Just go, get back to the shuttles."

"I owe you, Sam," Hondo said. "We'll get you back, too."

"I don't think I've got any balls left," he said, matter-of-factly.

He turned his head, and Hondo could see half of his face was gone as well, as if it was melted wax.

"We'll get you new ones," BK told him. "Hush."

Despite the darkness, Hondo could see the glint of tears in her eyes.

"If I do get them, then . . ." his voice trailed off before he quietly said, "BK, I'm afraid."

"I know you are . . ." she started before Sam's head lolled back.

He was gone.

"BK, we've got to go," Hondo said.

"I know. Give me a moment."

Hondo nodded. Another minute or two wouldn't make any difference.

"Dodds, move out" Sergeant Mbangwa's voice came over BK's PICS' external speakers. "We're falling in with the Brothers."

Hondo looked up in shock. He hadn't realized that her PICS was intact. She'd molted just to be with Sam. Once molted in the field, it would take an armorer to get her PICS functional gain.

BK lifted Sam off her lap, then stepped up to her PICS, hitting the mic and saying, "Roger. I've got Hondo with me, but Sam didn't make it."

"Most of us didn't make it," he responded with bitterness in his voice. "But I'm glad McKeever's with you. Look, we've got 30 minutes to get to Ozark. I'll see you there."

Ozark was an emergency LZ about four klicks away, nothing to a Marine in a PICS, but it could be tough going in their longjohns.

"Roger, that," she passed. "See you there."

"Ozark. We'd better get going," Hondo said.

She nodded, then bent over to pick up Sam's body.

"Let me," Hondo said.

BK could be stubborn, especially if someone was insinuating that she couldn't pull her own weight. But at just over half Hondo's mass, she just didn't have his strength. She nodded, stepping back.

Hondo picked up what was left of Sam and slung him over his shoulders. The resurrection and regen rate for casualties in this war was abysmal, but despite the damage to his face, Sam's brain had been functional. If there were a chance of resurrection, it was worth taking.

With BK leading, the two took off running. It would have been touch and go anyway, and Sam's body would slow him down, but there wasn't even a question.

Marines don't leave Marines behind.

FS OSCAR DE SPAN

Chapter 11
Hondo

Hondo flopped into his rack, still in his longjohns. He locked his eyes on the bottom of Sam's rack, 40 centimeters in front of his nose. It should have sunk under his friend's weight, creaking as he shifted his body. Only that wasn't going to happen anymore.

He refused to look anywhere else, not willing to take in the empty racks, racks that had been occupied not 22 hours earlier by his squadmates, his friends. Sam was gone. Brute was gone. Tara, Star Bright, and Josiah. Corporals Kleinmaster and Uheap. All gone.

Hondo had been a Marine for almost three years, during which time he'd barely heard shots in anger fired until the first fight against the Grubs. The squad had escaped unscathed then, and while he knew some of those who'd been killed, they'd been in other units. This time, though, for the first time during his service, his own squadmates had died, probably beyond resurrection.

Sam, Josiah, and Corporal Uheap had been put into stasis until the docs could figure out how to reverse the damage done to their bodies, but that was not a sure thing. Hondo had to consider them gone.

We weren't even supposed to be leading the fight!

There was a creak from the rack across from him.

"You OK, BK?" he asked.

She didn't respond, turning on her side and presenting her back to him.

Give her time. She and Sam . . .

The debrief had been brutal as well, but at least they'd been together, not going in individually. It wasn't as if anyone was being blamed for the loss, but the debriefers were digging in at the facts surrounding the ambush. Hondo understood why. The Grubs didn't show a lot of technology as humans understood it, and no one was quite sure just how intelligent they were or if they were acting by instinct—or, from what Hondo gathered, as some sort of hive mind.

The fact that they could power-down a PICS should have been an indication that these were not simply large animals, that and the fact that they could navigate space. Hondo hadn't any doubt about their intelligence, but the way they conducted their ambush cemented it. They adjusted to the tactical scenario as it unfolded. The Grubs were smart, and they could adapt. That made them more dangerous than the Capys had ever been and more dangerous than the Klethos.

Of course, they're more dangerous than the Klucks. That's why they came to us for help.

He still didn't understand what happened with Third Squad, though. The Klethos just didn't seem to have their heart in the fight. They'd been so deadly in the first few battles with humans not only because they had to tech to render human weapons useless, but they were so laser-focused on the battle. That wasn't what he'd seen on the planet, and he didn't know why.

Hondo was exhausted, but he couldn't sleep, his mind racing through the battle. The feeling of helplessness when he lost power had hit him hard. He'd always known that being a Marine came with risks. He understood that he could die, but that had always been an almost substanceless concept. With a useless PICS and a Grub bearing down on him, though, that had brought everything into focus. Hondo McKeever knew at that instant that he was mortal, and he was afraid.

The Grubs were a mortal danger, not just to him, not just to BK laying in the next rack, but to humanity as a whole. BK wanted revenge, and she wouldn't stop until she had it. Hondo felt differently. He did not want to face another Grub, but he would. If he didn't, someone else would have to, and if that person didn't, well, humanity would not survive.

PURGAMENTIUM

Chapter 12
Skylar

Sky was numb, and not just because of being up for 42 hours. Everything: the lack of sleep, the rush of adrenaline when the attack kicked off, and the horrible consequences of so many lives lost, had all taken its toll even before the marathon after action brief which showed no signs of ending soon.

She took another swig of Joltz, but the energy drink was losing its effectiveness. Pretty soon, she was going to have to go to something stronger if she was going to contribute.

Not that she had contributed much so far. This brief was being run by Archbishop Lowery himself, and all the department heads on the planet, as well as various worthies via meson-conferencing, were in attendance. Sky was definitely on the low end of the feeding scale, and she was there to answer questions, nothing more. After twelve hours, she'd been asked a grand total of two of them: one to repeat a finding from the Jesuits that she knew Janus had at his fingertips, and one on a vague question that had no known answer.

She tried to follow what was going on, but her mind kept drifting to the poor souls back on the planet. The Confederation battalion had essentially been wiped out to a man, and she'd held so much hope for the synchrotron particle beam projectors, something about which she'd become an advocate. The beams should have interrupted the cellular messaging of the Dictymorphs, but the soldiers had only managed to bring down one of them, and that one possibly because of cruder physical damage to its body.

She'd been an early advocate of the projectors, and now she felt an overwhelming sense of guilt.

They should have worked, she thought for the thousandth time.

The Jesuits, building on what others had begun, had finally come up with a biological model that seemed to fit observations. The Dictymorphs were not exactly individual organisms as she'd first thought, but neither were they a colony organism. When needed, they could detach energy-rich portions of themselves which could function on their own. The spheres rising from the main bodies were examples of this. These spheres had minimal mass, but a tremendous amount of stored energy. This energy could then be released as a type of organic artillery. In other words, they could "throw" parts of themselves through the air to extend their reach. How sentient the calved sections were or if the main body could communicate with them was open to debate, but they weren't "dumb bombs."

Within the Dictymorphs, their cells communicated with each other through a chemical process that flowed through the cell walls as quickly as impulses flowed through human or Klethos nerves. The scientist in her was fascinated by this. In some ways, this was superior to a nervous system. If a major nerve in a human being is cut, paralysis is the result. If you slice through a Dictymorph, then the chemical messaging can simply flow around the severed area until the adjacent cells were able to close the wound back together.

While fascinating, the teams' job was to find a way to defeat them, not marvel at their biology. One of the proposed weapons was the projectors carried by the Confed soldiers which were based, on a theoretical level, on the Klethos pikes.

These were supposed to interfere with the chemical messaging and halt the cellular data streams, and it worked in all their simulations. The Dictymorphs should not have been able to stand up to them.

Should have, would have.

The bottom line was that they hadn't, and soldiers died—and she contributed to that. An hour ago, the Confederation consul himself had gone ballistic over the conference feed, and Sky had sunk down in her seat, hoping not to be seen and just letting her seniors take the blast.

The consul had signed off, turning his representation over to a lower, but still lofty worthy, and now the debate was focused on the poor showing of the Klethos during the battle.

Sky had been surprised by that. They didn't flee the battle or something drastic, but they just hadn't fought with the same ferocious intent as they'd previously exhibited. The two separate Klethos battalions had brought down five of the Dictymorphs, suffering significant losses, but the integrated Klethos had done next to nothing.

Not quite. They might have killed one with three more driven off.

A Federation colonel had the floor, and he was ranting about the Klethos turning soft, and if they'd just have been more aggressive, then the battle would not have turned into the rout it was.

Given the topic, Sky didn't think anyone was going to call on her. She might be considered one of the foremost experts on the Klethos, but she was in the Dictymorph division. She pulled up one of the battle scenes on her PA, running through it several times. The Klethos squads with the Marines weren't shirking. The fighters moved in, taking the fight to the Dictymorphs, but there wasn't any of the determination they simply oozed whenever they'd fought before. It didn't make sense.

When something didn't make sense, Sky had to worry it like a terrier on a rat, trying to pull out the connection.

The Klethos, at least the warrior class and the d'relle, seemed to have two speeds. The first was a calm, almost lackadaisical demeanor. Not much seemed to excite them. Their second speed was the running-amok warrior whose only goal was to destroy the enemy. For the d'relle, they seemed to express this groove through their hakas, as if they had too much energy to contain. It also probably served to strike fear into their opponents and gave battle the ritualistic factor that the Klethos loved. The warrior class also had their more formalized versions of the haka, but there were other rituals they performed, previously unobserved by humans. In many ways, it seemed as if the warriors were kept deep inside of each Klethos, where they wouldn't interfere with Klethos-lee daily life. The warrior aspect was then summoned forth like a demon, ready to rend and kill when needed, and announced their arrivals through the sheer exuberance of their dance.

Sky asked her AI to splice together a feed on the Klethos that left nothing out, then sped through it in reverse, trying to see something, anything, that might account for their lack of ferocity. There wasn't anything, not from their appearance in the hangar bay through the launch down to the planet, not from the assembly area through the attack. Nothing stuck out at her.

Maybe what isn't there is the problem? What am I missing?

She set the feed back to the beginning, fast forwarding it again, the figures jerkily dancing in their sped-up motion.

Dancing?

Something tugged at her mind, and with an almost audible snap, it fell into place. They hadn't danced at all. There had been no *lisspyth,* or what the humans called their haka.

As far as she knew, the Klethos always performed a haka before battle, but the eight Klethos she followed, of which only one had survived, none had danced.

Unless they did it before they got to the hangar? No, that doesn't make sense. Too early.

The accepted theory for the Jekyll-Hyde thing the Klethos warriors had going was to ensure social compatibility. It could be difficult for a society to get along if crazed warriors were always in the mix. Sky had once read a student's dissertation, however, that postulated that the physical drain of the warrior state was not something that could be kept up indefinitely. Male elephants in musth burned an inordinate number of calories, so the Klethos warrior "musth" could have the same effect. They turned it on and off as an evolutionary tool to save energy.

That made sense to Sky, and if that student had been correct, then that Klethos squad would not have warriored-up while still up on the ship. So why didn't they later on the planet's surface, and did that account for their lack of alacrity during the attack?

She switched to one of the two Klethos battalions, following them from their arrival en masse at their LZ through the battle and to the departure of the survivors. As they approached the Line of Departure, a percentage of the Klethos seemed to make abortive jumps and gestures that looked like abbreviated hakas as if only part of their warrior had emerged.

Lieutenant Colonel Boswell, did we give the Klethos orders not to perform their hakas?

Two rows in front of her, the Federation officer picked up his PA, then looked around, finally catching her eyes.

Not exactly. We told them they couldn't take the time. We had to take the fight to the Grubs immediately after landing, but I never paid attention to that, he wrote back to her. *We're trying to keep them in mutually supportable formations while not giving the Grubs time to react. Why?*

Nothing yet. Just working on a theory. I'll get back to you.

She was getting close to something, a thought that fluttered like a moth just beyond the reach of the candle's light. If the Klethos hadn't been specifically forbidden to perform their haka, then something else was happening. She should have seen more of the little jumps and gestures among the fighters. But since they hadn't, she had to think that they didn't dance because they were not in their warrior mode. But why weren't they? That was the million-credit question.

Unless . . . she paused, trying to will her subconscious to reveal itself.

Unless the haka is not a sign of their warrior self but the cause of it?

She paused again as her heart rate bumped up.

It can't be that easy.

Maori warriors of old used hakas to put fear into their enemies, but it was also used to get the adrenaline flowing, to pump up the blood. Rugby players around the galaxy kept the practice alive over the centuries.

What if the haka is not a sign that they are ready? What it if isn't something that merely helps the process? What if it is necessary?

Sky felt the certainty that she was on the right track, and she needed more data input than her PA could easily give her. She needed full access to the research AIs. Mindless of the debate still raging and suddenly flush with more energy than ten bottles of Joltz could have given her, she got up from her seat and slid out of the conference hall.

If she was right, then by forcing the Klethos into the human military mold, they were dooming them to failure.

Chapter 13
Skylar

Skylar stared at "Diane," trying to read from the d'solle's face what she was thinking.

Archbishop Lowery, who was sitting beside her, had gone out on a limb for her on this, breaking the impasse between EC Baker and Peyton Janus. Janus had rejected her theory after only a cursory glance, telling her to get her focus back on the Dictymorphs. Baker, on the other hand, had seen merit in it, and after consultation with the military staff, decided to take it to the archbishop. The archbishop thought there was enough there to warrant an approach the Klethos command quad to get their feedback.

This had been the first time Sky had been the main speaker at such a high-level meeting within the task force, and she'd been more than a little nervous. She was working from conjecture, after all, and she could be wrong. If her fellow humans thought she was wrong, the worse that could happen was that she'd be fired and sent home. But they were dealing with an alien race, aliens in an alliance that was not doing well. Sky didn't know if the quad would agree with her premise, and if they didn't, what their reaction might be.

Sky was sure, now, that the hakas and other battle formalities were needed for them to reach the degree of force of will necessary to achieve battlefield success. By forcing the proverbial square peg in the round hole, the square peg was useless and the hole remained unfilled.

Over the last day, while Sky and the others argued the concept, the military shifted to her view. The problem with that vision, however, was that hyped-up Klethos warriors in a battle frenzy would have a difficult time in fighting alongside more level-headed humans. As Lieutenant Colonel Boswell said, if her theory were true, then mixed units would be both impractical and a liability.

The recommendation of the workgroup was to keep human units human and Klethos unit Klethos, but fight them complimenting each other. Let the humans come up with the tactical plan and provide secondary forces with the Klethos becoming the shock forces to crush the Dictymorphs.

This has hardly been a unanimous recommendation. Janus had crafted a strong dissent, signed by Dr. Creighton Spiller, Sky's counterpart in the Klethos division.

Now that she'd finished her presentation to the quad, Sky wondered if they'd been right. An impartial observer could take her theory as an insult to the honor-driven Klethos. In some ways, she was inferring that the highly-advanced Klethos were savages of some sort, incapable of the understanding martial arts. The Klethos had come to the humans for assistance, yet she was advocating that they fight not only in separate maneuver units, but that they bear the brunt of the danger. The more she looked at the unmoving d'solle, the more she was afraid that Janus had been right.

The pause grew longer, uncomfortably long, before Diane asked, "It is your contention that humans and Klethos cannot effectively serve in integrated units?"

"Yes, ma'am," she said, reverting to a junior-senior posture despite the fact that honorifics were not used with the Klethos.

Her nose began to itch something awful, but she refused to lift her hand to scratch it.

"Furthermore, you believe that the Klethos-lee need to conduct *lisspyth* in order to effectively battle the *kshree*," she asked, using the Klethos term for the Dictymorphs, a sound that was more of a click and whistle than anything a human throat could make."

Sky looked around as if looking for help, but she was on her own here. If she was wrong, no one was going to come to her rescue.

"Yes, that is our theory, based on limited observations," she said. "If we are in any way mistaken, we would welcome your input."

"Please wait while we contemplate this revelation."

Humans were not sure when a d'rolle said "we" if that was the royal "we" or if a quad could somehow communicate between themselves without speaking.

At least she didn't erupt in anger, she thought. *Still time for that, though.*

She risked a glance at the rest of the humans. When she caught Lieutenant Colonel Boswell's eyes, he gave her a slow wink.

"Doctor Ybarra, what you have just said is very revealing. We wish there to be no misunderstanding, so if I may paraphrase your telling, humans only now know the essence of *lisspyth* to the Klethos-lee?"

Sky looked around again, waiting for someone to jump in. Diane, as did all Klethos with contact with humans, spoke excellent Standard, but that didn't mean there was complete understanding. Words had meaning, but so did inflection, body language, and tone, none of which the Klethos used in ways that conveyed meaning to humans.

"This is the theory now, yes."

"We do not understand," she said.

Sky was about to try and rephrase the theory when the Klethos d'rolle continued, "The *lisspyth* is our very essence, no more or less as is breathing. We need the *lisspyth* in order to function. How you cannot understand this after more than a century of your years is beyond comprehension. Your Ryck

Lysander understood it. Your gladiators understood it. How can you not?"

The archbishop cleared his throat, and for a moment, Sky thought he was going to jump in, but when he didn't, she said, "We know of the *lisspyth*," she said, her voice catching on the sibilant S's. "We have much the same with our hakas. But they are not part of our *essence*, as you say. They are . . . they're a celebration, a warning, sometimes."

There was another uncomfortably long pause, then, "You have given us much to contemplate. How can a *lisspyth* not be an essence? But that answers a question. We've been unable to understand why you humans want to handicap our warrior class. This may be the answer."

Handicap? They've been thinking we wanted to handicap them?

"Ma'am, if we are handicapping your warriors, why did you agree to that?" she asked.

"Our war with the *kshree* is not going well. Unless something changes, there can be only one outcome. You humans are the only race we know with honor . . ."

There was a flurry of tiny motions from several of the seated humans as they accessed PAs, and Sky knew why. According to what they'd been told by both the Trinoculars and the Klethos, the Klethos had eliminated 17 other species of intelligent life. Unless Diane meant the meager remnants of the Trinoculars, she could have just revealed that there were still other intelligent species out there.

". . . and our d'rolle decided to approach you to discover if you can be the instrument of the change that can signal our survival."

When she said "d'rolle," there was a subtle difference in the word, and both the linguists and the AIs would be analyzing that to death, Sky knew.

"We came to you asking for assistance, and if you believed that we needed to handicap our warriors, in honor, we had to agree and carry out the experiment."

"But your warriors have been getting slaughtered," Colonel Ng said.

"Our warriors have been dying ever since we pulled ourselves out of the primordial swamp, Colonel. But yes, our losses have been dramatic without inflicting more damage upon the *kshree*."

"How long would you have continued like this," Sky asked. "Fighting without your *lisspyth*?"

"Our recall, and the ceasing of cooperation, Doctor, was imminent."

"And now?" she asked, her breath caught in her throat and afraid of the response.

"That recall is now on hold. We wish to see how your segregated maneuver units can achieve success."

A deathly silence fell over the room.

Shit, they were about to pull out.

Sky knew that a large percentage of humanity would welcome that. They didn't agree to the war, and they wanted humans out of the fight. Sky knew, however, that would only postpone the inevitable. The Dictymorphs, the Grubs, as the troops called them, would one day reach human space. Humanity's best chance lay with allying with the Klethos-lee and together, defeating the threat.

"Diane," the archbishop said, taking over from Sky. "I am glad to know that our effort is still to be ongoing. I thank you and your team for taking the time to meet with us. We are going to break away and come up with a more detailed plan. I trust if my team has questions, they may contact you?"

"We are here for that reason, Archbishop."

"Very well. In that case, let's close this meeting. I will personally keep you informed," he said rising to his feet.

Diane nodded, and in unison, the entire quad rose, and in their fashion, left the room without the social pleasantries that humans loved.

As soon as they hatch door closed behind them, the Archbishop turned first to the pick-up on the table and asked, "Lauralee, did you get all of that?"

Lauralee? As in Tsagaanbaatar, the UAM Secretary General? She was listening to me speak? Sky wondered in awe.

"Yes, I got it all," the voice out of the speaker said. "Very interesting development. I'll have Harris brief the heads of state. Oh, Doctor Ybarra, can you hear me?"

"Yes, ma'am, I can hear you," Sky said, her heart racing.

"Good job, very good job."

Sky was gobsmacked as she stuttered out her thanks.

"We've got a lot of work to do and not much time. This is within our charter, so we won't need HOS approval for this. Terrence, Caesar, I want you two to honcho this personally," he told EC Baker and General Reicker. "Get a working group together and give me something by fifteen hundred tomorrow that I can forward to the Grand Council."

The room immediately went into motion as people were called in for the working group. Sky hovered, ready and able, but while Janus was selected for the group, she was left standing.

"Kind of sucks, huh? This was all your idea, and now the big kids want to take over," Lieutenant Colonel Boswell said as he stepped up beside her. "Not to worry, I'm not playing varsity on this one, either."

"But you know more about Klethos tactics than anyone here, Colonel," Sky said, surprised to hear he wasn't on the working group either.

"If you can call that they do tactics, you mean," he said. "And if you don't mind, you can call me Bill. I know that technically you're my senior, me being but a lowly O5, but seeing as we keep bumping into each other, it might be easier."

Knowing how anal the Marines could be about rank, she looked at the colonel in surprise, but his big smile told her he was not quite as hidebound as some officers could be.

"Sure, Bill. That would be nice."

He cocked his head at her and raised his eyebrows in a question.

"Oh, and you can call me Skylar. Or Sky, as my friends call me."

"Sky it is, then. Well, seeing as how we didn't get picked for the big leagues, I think I could use a good cup of espresso. The Confed Staff NCO's got a hold of a D'Longhi machine, and I've been hankering to see if it's as good as they say. If I had you with me running interference, I bet they'd allow let a Federation Marine have a cup. What say you?"

Sky had been running on empty for the last 20 hours, but she felt that she should be doing something. She was here to decipher the Dictymorphs, after all, not the Klethos, and she'd been neglecting that. But as she looked at the Lieutenant . . . at Bill, with a bad-boy twinkle in his eyes, she thought *screw it*.

"What say me? I say lead on, Bill. Let's see if we can sweet talk them into a cup."

Chapter 14
Hondo

"So, we're not getting new Klucks?" Lance Corporal Roosevelt Jesus River Molina asked.

"We lost seven of them. Only Boudica made it out, Rosy," Hondo said.

"Still, we lost . . ." the big Marine started before trailing off.

"We lost seven of us, you mean," Loren said quietly. "And now we're being brought up to speed."

"Well, yeah, I guess."

"The word is that the Klucks are going to be kept to their own units. That's what the sergeant says," Hondo told them.

"I mean, I don't give a shit, but they did kill that second Grub. Just kept up the assault until the thing collapsed," Loren said. "So why take them away now?"

"The rumor is that we're holding them down, you know. Like we keep them from going ballistic on the Grubs."

"Isn't that what we've been trying to do for the last five months? I mean, keep them in check and teach them how to fight as units?" she persisted.

"That's what we've been doing, yeah. But you saw them, Loren. It was like they were sleepwalking. I don't know. Maybe they're right. Maybe the Klucks have got to do their own thing," Hondo said.

"Maybe. I don't know. I do know that I don't like the newbies coming in," she whispered, glancing to the new

Marines stowing their gear at the far end of their squadbay. "I'd have rather merged with Second Squad."

Hondo understood her point. He didn't know the new Marines who'd only just been assigned to the squad that morning. He knew, and more importantly, trusted the Marines from Second. They'd gone through the shit together.

"So, you're gonna have one squad with all combat vets and two all-newbie squads? Yeah, right, that's a sterling idea," Rosy said.

"Oh, I know. I'm just saying."

Hondo looked over at the newbies from where the three of them—four if he counted BK asleep in the rack beside him—were huddled. The three privates looked young, very young. But there was a PFC and a lance corporal as well. They were all probably good Marines, but he just didn't know that yet, and a good leader knew his people.

Hondo had to be a good leader, now. Corporal Yetter was taking over First, and he'd be getting only the newbies to fill out the team. Hondo was taking over Second Team, and along with BK, would be receiving two of them.

He wasn't sure how much training time they'd have, but one thing was a certainty. Sometime in the near future, he'd have to lead his team into combat.

He hoped he'd be ready.

Chapter 15
Skylar

"I think you're missing the point, Lars," Sky said. "The mirror shields are not a weapon. I understand what you're saying about the Roman scutum being used offensively, but do you really think a Dictymorph is going to fall to one? No, L'Teesha's right. We've seen that there is still a degree of reflectance in the taraline—"

"But not the dielectric mirrors," he interrupted.

"No, not the dielectric. But we're not here to discuss what doesn't work, but rather what does. And the taraline mirrors were able to reflect back a significant portion of the tendrils."

Sky and eight others were at the children's table, discussing shielding, while the adults in the larger conference room were working on offensive weapons. Her brief brush with notoriety with her theory on the Klethos had long faded, and she was back to peon level. She wasn't sure why she was even here. She was a xenopsychologist, not a physicist. Lars Skagt, with his specialty in ancient weapons, was like a bulldog with his shield theory. Sky now knew more about scutums, clipeus, and how the umbo, the metal bosses on the scutums, were used to pound on opponents than she'd ever thought she'd know.

Which had no relevance to the issue. The Legionnaires who'd been carrying the different types of mirror shields had been test cases, guinea pigs, as it were, just as the Confederation troops with their synchrotron particle beam projectors. They were testing theory, not practical weapons.

Didn't matter to the poor Confed soldiers. They're all just as dead one way or the other.

She shook her head to get back on track. Lars was driving everyone crazy, a super-specialist trying to find relevance. L'Teesha Durrant-Kubrick, a quiet, but brilliant theoretical engineer, had the data to back up the partial effectiveness of the taraline mirrors, something that hadn't been given much credence before the test.

Battle, not test, Sky. People died.

As brilliant as L'Teesha was, she had the aggressiveness of a one-day-old kitten, and she was letting Lars walk all over her. Sky, even without a background in the field, wasn't going to let that happen. Lives of the soldiers mattered more than professional ego.

"Not all of the tendrils, though," Lars continued.

"Something is better than nothing, Doctor Skagt. If we can increase the soldiers' survival by even ten seconds, that could be enough to use the pikes and kill one of the things. The key here is the taraline, not the shield," Shy said in her best professor-voice.

"But the scutums can do that. They can give the soldiers the time, too," he insisted.

"Look, Skagt," she said, standing as frustration took over. "Until the Dictymorph reaches right around it. And with one hand holding a shield, one hand on a pike, how does a soldier use another weapon, huh? If you'd seen a Dictymorph up close, if you'd felt death closing in on you, then you'd understand."

Which wasn't quite fair. Lars had never been offered a chance to make a landing, so she didn't know if he would have volunteered or not. Everyone knew she'd been on the ground during the first battle, and she was going to take any advantage she had if it moved the effort forward.

"No, we are not here to discuss shields. Our takeaway from this is going to be to recommend polished taraline plating to be attached to combat suits, just as Doctor Durrant-Kubrick suggested. L'Teesha, I assume you can write that up?"

"Yes, I already have it," she said with a look of gratitude in her eyes.

"OK, then. Item 2002 is finished. We've got five more items on the list for today and two hours to get through them. So, Item 2003, the effects of heat. Enos, I think this is yours. If you would begin?"

Sky was not in charge of the meeting. She was barely more than an observer given the items on the agenda, and wished she was back in the lab working on any one of six or seven projects on her to-do list. But if it took someone to ride herd on the others, then she was going to step up into the saddle.

Chapter 16
Hondo

"You look like the Silent Knight," BK said, laughing at him.

Hondo put his opened right gauntlet over his heart, the slowly rotated his hand away, giving his heart to the people, just at the Silent Knight did after every act of derring-do.

He did sort of look like the Hollybolly hero of a dozen or so flicks, his armor a shiny, reflective silver. They all looked like him. A PICS was a war machine, designed to close with and kill the enemy. It was not designed as a target. Besides passive stealth measure, it had active jamming, even to human eyes. The fractured array could interfere with an observer's ability to process what he or she saw. An enemy might know the PICS was there but couldn't pinpoint it.

Now, most of his PICS' exterior surface was covered in bright taraline surfaces that angled in unexpected shapes. The scientists swore that these mirrors would reflect at least a portion of the Grub's weaponry, giving them up to twenty seconds of protection instead of the five seconds a regular PICS gave him.

His thought drifted back to K-1003 for a moment. With twenty seconds, maybe Brute would have been able to break free. Maybe he would, and Sam would still be alive.

Maybe, maybe, maybe.

He shook his head as if to shake out those thoughts. He couldn't dwell on the past.

Private Fiona Xeras, his new team rifleman, pivoted on her left foot, turning a complete 360, then strutted down the front of the armory as if on the catwalk. Hondo stifled a laugh.

Somehow, in her PICS, she captured the caricature of the runway model.

"Can it, Xeras," BK said. "We don't have time for your grab-assing. We still need to get down to the range and get up-checked."

BK didn't seem to like the private, and she rode her pretty hard. Hondo didn't know if that was because Xeras had filled Sam's billet as rifleman or if there was something more involved. Hondo was new to this leadership thing, and as BK hadn't stepped over the line with anything yet, he'd let it slide so far. He'd love to talk with Yetter or Mbangwa about it, to pick their brains, but he didn't want to seem as if he couldn't handle anything so minor. He knew, though, that he'd have to talk to BK about it at some point.

"Let's get going. Time's tight," he told the other three.

His PICS felt subtly different than his original combat suit, even before the new armor plating. Now, the difference was magnified. He couldn't put his finger on exactly what was different, but just as two pairs of jeans, both the same size, felt different then he put them on, so did his new PICS differ from his old one.

Range 401 was about 500 meters behind the armory. It was a cold range, meaning no live fire. CWO4 Donaldson was sending another Marine through his paces while Staff Sergeant Jardine monitored the readouts.

The two Marines looked exhausted. They'd been at is since zero-dark-thirty, and now it was almost evening chow time. Hondo doubted they'd left the range all day other than to take a piss break. The Marine being tested completed the vertical jump, coming back down a little hard, but within reason. The gunner looked at the staff sergeant who gave him a thumbs up. He gave the Marine a slap on the hip, and pointed off the range.

"Hell, we've got eight in front of us. I know we're going to miss chow," BK said.

"They'll keep it. Gunny promised," Hondo reminded her.

"We'll see," she said, not sounding too optimistic.

As far as Hondo was concerned, if Gunny Harris said chow was going to remain open for them, then that was set in stone. The gunny stood all of 1.7 meters in his socks, but nobody wanted to get on his bad side, and that included the civilian mess staff.

Hondo reached out and grabbed BK by the shoulder, twisting her so he could see her back. She knocked his arm away.

"How're you going to put your good luck charm on with the mirrors?" he asked.

BK was on the superstitious side, and she'd put a small four-leaf clover patch on the back shoulder of her PICS. That PICS was abandoned back on K-1003 when she'd molted, and she hadn't yet put one on her new PICS. Hondo figured that was because she'd been waiting for her new PICS to get up-armored.

"Don't think I'm gonna do it," she said.

"What? But that's your good luck charm," he protested.

"Didn't bring good luck before, huh?" she muttered.

"You came back in one piece," he said. "You've got to remember that."

She didn't reply, and the two friends stood in silence while waiting their turn. When they reached the front of the queue, Hondo watched Xeras, BK, and PFC Sunrise Valúlfur go through their paces before he stepped up to the chief warrant officer.

The gunner scanned his PICS' id, did a circuit reading, then told Hondo to bend over, followed by standing on each leg separately, running in place, running in a circle, jumping over the simulated creek, and a dozen other exercises. The PICS handled well, nothing much out of the ordinary. After he completed the vertical jump for height, the gunner looked back to Jardine.

The more detailed analysis must have been fine because he said, "OK, Lance Corporal McKeever. You're good to go. I'm up-checking you."

Hondo joined his three waiting Marines, then together, they jogged back to the armory to get out of their suits and to the messhall. They could have walked, but despite the Gunny's promises, there was no use tempting fate when chow was concerned.

Chapter 17
Hondo

"Look at those fuckers," BK said as if she couldn't believe it.

Hondo sure couldn't.

Images of rioting filled the screen while an on-site reporter described what was going on. It was pretty obvious, though. The mob was decrying the war, decrying violence, and rioting to prove their point that violence was a bad thing. Behind the reporter, a young man and woman emerged from the broken window of a storefront, carrying a large box between them.

"Take a look at that. Yeah, stealing a holoprojector is a good way to protest the war," Loren said, wrinkling her face in disgust.

"Don't they know that if we don't stop the Grubs, they'll be coming for us next?"

"Yeah, in a hundred years, so it doesn't matter now, right?" Hondo said.

He didn't understand it, either. He'd thought that all of humanity was behind the effort. Over the last month, 22,000 new fighters, mostly from the Big 3, but also from smaller governments, had arrived on the planet for training.

Yet every day, as the non-rates watched the news, more and more protests were cropping up. This one was on Syble-3, right in the heart of the Confederation.

The reporter snagged a man and asked him why he was protesting.

"It just ain't right, man. Us and the Klethos together? I mean, look at them. They're Satan's spawn, and it don't take no genius to figure that one out."

"Surely you mean that figuratively."

"Yeah, I figure it, and you should, too. I mean, lookit, them Klethos, they killed out 17 species. Seventeen! They woulda done in the Capys too, if we hadn't stepped in."

"Who's this idiot?" BK asked.

"And now, they tried for more'n a hundred years to get us, too. Only we're too strong for them, so they're trying something new."

"We were too 'strong' for the Klethos?" the reporter asked, incredulity creeping into his normal reporter-neutral voice.

"He's right in that, at least," Rosy said.

Hondo wasn't so sure about that. The Klethos showed little tactical skill, but they still could neutralize human weaponry. As the man said, they'd killed off 17 other races, and they didn't do that by being pushovers.

"Yeah. I saw on the holovid that we've got more planets now than we did when we first ran into them. How can we do that if we aren't winning with the gladiators? Just make a million gladiators, and we'd wipe the Klethos out of the galaxy."

"So, sir, be that as it may, why are you protesting now? It isn't the Klethos we're fighting."

"No, it ain't. But maybe it should be. How do we know these Dicty-things are the bad guys?"

"They just killed 845 Confederation soldiers, for one thing."

"Because we attacked, them. I seen the holovids. And if they really are the bad guys, then maybe we shouldn't draw a target on our backs. Now, they'll come gunning for us."

The reporter looked stunned, as if he couldn't believe what the man had said.

"Well, thank you, sir, for taking the time to talk to us."

"No problem," he said, then looked right into the holocorder, leaned in, and said, "All of you out there, you've got to get your head out of your asses. This ain't our fight."

He raised his hand in a fist, his fore and little finger raised.

"There you have it. One citizen's views on the war with the Dictymorphs," the reporter said.

"Do you think his views are widespread?" the anchor asked.

"It's hard to say. All I know is that is the general feeling of those here, the ones doing the rioting."

"It will be interesting seeing what the UAM Grand Council will say about it now. There is only a week left for the continuing resolution," the anchor said. "Keep an eye on the situation for us on Syble-3, Harold, but stay safe."

The image shifted to the anchor back in the studio on FRL Station.

"With all the unrest that is spreading throughout human space, just what is the Grand Council thinking now. We've got five distinguished guests here to discuss—"

"There," BK said, turning off the feed. "I'm about done with that kind of shit. Fucking Confeds, anyway."

Hondo didn't bother to mention that there were protests on Federation worlds as well. BK had taken Sam's death hard, and he thought she at least partly blamed the Confederation battalion for that.

"Ain't no thing. The galaxy's full of idiots," Kilter said. "We just do our duty, like we always do, protecting the citizens."

"Yeah, we do," BK said. "Even if they don't always deserve it."

The breakroom was quiet for a moment, the Marines lost in thought.

"Come on, BK, let's hit Ice and Fire," Hondo said, breaking the silence. "I think you owe me about a billion credits now."

"Ain't a billion." She pulled out her PA, then said, "Eight-hundred-forty-three million, two-hundred-and-two-thousand, one-hundred and four, to be exact."

"You owe him that much, BK?" Kilter said, hooting with laughter. "You've got to be the shittiest player in the Corps. Hell, that'll take you a thousand years to pay him off with that salary."

"I ain't gonna be a lance coolie forever. I'll make corporal, then pay him off with my raise," she said.

Hondo pulled out the deck from the drawer, then dangled it in front of her.

"Here's your chance to knock some off of your debt."

She swatted at the deck, which he jerked out of the way.

They used to play with Sam but hadn't played since K-1003.

"Come on, or are you afraid of losing more?"

She glared at him for a moment, then shrugged. "Deal, then, if you're so dead set on losing."

"I'm in," shouted several voices as they scrambled to take chairs.

"Eight cards, dragons wild," Hondo said as he shuffled the deck.

BK's eyes sparkled with intensity as the Marines forgot about politics and focused on what was really important.

Chapter 18
Skylar

"No kidding? I never heard anything about it," Sky asked Bill, who'd just stuck his head in the lab to tell her.

"I think they wanted to keep it a secret," he told her. "Well, are you going to put down saving the galaxy for a few minutes and come and see?"

Sky hesitated, looking down at the 10,000-word treatise on Dictymorph risk aversion. She still had to clean it up, maybe another four hours of work. This was her 32nd report. All were submitted, and the best she could tell, all were simply filed away. Not that she blamed anyone. She was shooting in the dark here, hoping she'd hit something. As if anyone understood Dictymorph risk aversion? There just wasn't anything close to the data available to even begin to analyze the subject. But they wanted something on risk aversion, so they got it.

They're just going to have to wait, she suddenly decided.

"Hell, yeah, I'm coming," she said, powering down her link. "Where are they?"

"At the flagpole," Bill said. "At least they were when I came to find you."

"You didn't have to do that," she said. "You could have stopped there."

"I knew you'd have your nose in some report that no one would ever read, so I thought I'd rescue you."

"Hey, someone reads these," she protested.

What he said was closer to the truth, but she didn't want to admit it. She'd had her one flash in the pan with the Klethos, but she doubted that she'd contributed much of anything about the Dictymorphs.

"Yeah, right. You keep telling yourself that."

People were streaming to the flagpole, coming from every direction. Sky despaired about getting close, but she forgot she had a Marine running interference.

"Make a hole, make a hole," Bill kept yelling, and surprising enough, people got out of his way.

I guess there's something to be said for that voice of command.

They turned the corner into the square, and over the heads of the gathered soldiers and civilians, she could see the four of them towering over the crowd.

The Federation's Mary Curnutte, the "Purple Sledgehammer." Jessria de Pontier, the "Bell," from Hospice Station. The Brotherhood's Shiloh Aprahamian, the "Silver Ice." From the Alliance of Free States, Krylie Fenster-Pan, the "Tungsten Claw." Four gladiators, all aces.

Sky knew that all, of course. Their hair, each with distinctive colors, marked them even more than their bulk. Seeing them on the holos, though, did not nearly have the same impact as seeing them in real life. Besides towering over three meters tall, they simply exuded power, something Sky could feel even 30 meters away.

Bill was making a herculean effort to get in closer, but even if people had wanted to let them pass, there was no room to get out of the way. Sky knew this was about as close as she was going to get.

The four gladiators were high-fiving, elbow-tapping, and fist-bumping everyone within reach—and they could reach a long ways with their wingspans. Sky felt like a little girl at her first bowy-bop concert, and she had to repress the urge to scream.

Not everyone was holding back. Screams and shouts echoed through the square as people tried to get closer or simply called out for attention.

Behind the gladiators, Sky could just see the heads of a dozen too-serious-looking men and women in black suits as if right out of central casting. Sky almost laughed—as if four gladiators needed UAM security for protection.

A large drone swept in closer, the UBS logo on its side. This was newsworthy, the first such event for close to two months that might interest viewers across human space.

"Ah, so that's it," Sky muttered as things fell into place.

The war had not been going well, and various factions wanted to end the effort. The UAM joint expedition needed a win, and needed one badly, but they hadn't fought since K-1003. More and more units were arriving on the growing base for training, but the newsies and documentary holomakers could only go to the ranges so many times before it got old and the viewing public lost interest.

The gladiators were rock stars, all of them, the best that humanity could produce. Each of them had survived five battles in the ring. The inclusion of the Tungsten Claw couldn't be ignored, either, from a political sense. The Alliance was making strong comments about how humanity should pull back to its own borders and not seek military "adventurism" in Klethos space. With one of their daughters on such public display, the UAM was making a political statement. Humanity was in this together.

The copper-haired Bell leaned back and down for a moment, and Sky saw a UAM staffer tilt his head up to say something to her. The Bell nodded, then the four gladiators pushed forward into the crowd, followed by the security. It was slow going, both because the people were packed in tight and because the gladiators kept up the high-fives. Sky and Bill pushed to their left on an intercept course, and as the gladiators came abreast of them, Sky lifted her hand, almost jumping on the back of a Brotherhood soldier to high-five Bell.

Bell was slapping the hands of everyone within reach, but she missed Sky's by a good ten centimeters.

"Damn, I didn't get it," she said, turning to face Bill.

"Why FS15 Ybarra, I'm surprised. You, a fangirl?" Bill said in mock solemnity.

"I saw you reaching up to try, too, Colonel, so don't give me that."

"Not to try, to succeed. I'm never going to wash my hand again," he said, holding it up to his face.

"You got a high-five?" she asked.

"More like a high-three, but that counts."

"Must be nice to have longer arms," she said reaching out to rub his hand. "There, now I got it, too, by proxy."

They both turned to watch the gladiators make their way to the headquarters, Sky on tiptoes as she tried to look over the heads of the massed people. It took almost five minutes for the gladiators to make it to the entrance, where they turned to wave at the crowd, then entered the building.

"That was pretty cool. First time I've ever seen a gladiator for real," she said as the crowd started to break up, people buzzing about what they'd just seen.

"My third time, but it doesn't get old," Bill said. "So, you going back to work?"

"Yeah . . ." she started before reconsidering.

She'd been putting out paper after paper based on conjecture, conjecture about which she had little confidence. She knew they were being read, but she didn't think they were contributing much to the cause. She could rush back, finish this one in another four hours, then put upload it to Janus' inbox where he might get to it tomorrow, maybe the next day, before deciding if it had enough merit to forward it on up the line. Sky prided herself on her sense of discipline, but she had to admit to herself that the galaxy wouldn't stop revolving around the center of the universe if she waited until tomorrow to get back to it.

She was feeling good, even a little giddy after seeing the gladiators. She simply didn't feel like going back to the lab.

"It's just past fourteen hundred. Is it too early for you to have a drink?" she asked Bill. "I'm buying."

"It's seventeen hundred somewhere, and that's good enough for me, especially if you're buying. The Club?"

The Club was the facility for field grade officers and civilian equivalents.

"No, I'm thinking of The Baiae," she said.

"The Baiae? Again you surprise me, but again, I say yes."

The Baiae, named after Nero's city of hedonism, was an unofficial club in Confedtown, run by the Confederation forces' SNCOs. It was run-down and somewhat grimy, but the drinks were cold, the snacks salty, and it was just the kind of place Sky felt like this afternoon.

"OK, then. I've got a feeling that more than a few people will be cutting off early and heading over, so we'd better get going."

"Allow me," he said, pushing in front of her, before bellowing out, "Make a hole, make a hole!"

Hmph. I guess he can be useful after all, she thought as she followed him to Confedtown.

Chapter 19
Hondo

"Chicken or rabbit," CWO5 Curnutte asked Hondo.

"Rabbit, ma'am," he answered holding out his tray.

"Fabricated rabbit, tasted like carboard when I was a private, tastes like cardboard now, too."

It wasn't that funny, but Hondo laughed—too loud. BK, who'd just been served, reached back to pull him along the line.

"Not too obvious, huh?" she said.

Hondo couldn't tear his eyes away from the huge gladiator. He would have loved to take a selfie with her, to send it back to his family on Paradhiso. Shona culture was very warrior-oriented, and his family would eat it up.

"Hockers, son?"

Hondo loved the purple beans, fabricated soft and chewy, so he said, "Yeah," his eyes still on the gladiator as she served the next Marine. He felt the plop of the beans on his plate and turned to step down the line when he saw who'd just served him.

"I mean, yes, sir. Thank you, sir!" to Colonel Oesper, the Marine brigade commander.

"She kind of sucks the air out of the room, right, lance corporal?" the colonel said with a smile.

"Uh . . . yes, sir," he said, barely getting the words out.

"Smooth move, Hondo," BK whispered. "Try not to disrespect the CO next."

Lieutenant Colonel Tan "Gunslinger" Rainer, the 3/6 commanding officer was the last server in line, handing out twist rolls to those who wanted them. They actually smelled delicious, as if actually baked, not popped out of the commercial fabricators that manufactured most of their food. Hondo managed to keep his composure as he accepted a roll, then followed BK to the table the squad had claimed as their rightful territory.

The officers and senior SNCOs often served the troops, usually on battalion patron days, the Marine Corps birthday, or other special occasions. Hondo had never been served by a gladiator, though, and that had thrown him off his game.

There was a loud crash, and Hondo turned to see one of the corporals, standing ash-faced, his tray on the ground in front of the Purple Sledgehammer.

"At least I'm not the only one," he muttered.

The company had been out at the infiltration range when the order had been given for them to return to base camp. Hondo had initially thought that they had a new mission, and a thrill of both excitement and fear coursed through him. Excitement because, quite frankly, he was getting bored with the training. Fear because he was now a leader, and he hoped he wouldn't screw up where someone could get killed because of it.

When they got back to camp, however, they found out the reason. The gladiators were on a visit, including CWO5 Curnutte. They'd all watched the broadcast of the pep talk given by some UAM bigwigs, General Reicker, and more importantly, the four gladiators. Hondo had been impressed that he was on the same planet as not just four of them at the same time, but four famous aces, one being a Marine, no less.

But to come into the messhall and see the gladiator, towering above the rest of the servers, had blown his mind. His brother would give his left nut to be this close to a gladiator ace.

Fuck it. Better to act and ask for forgiveness later.

"BK, take my PA," he said, unlocking it.

"What are you going to do?" she asked, immediately suspicious.

He reached over and opened the camera, then stood up and moved to the drink bar. He took a glass, filled it with the first drink in the dispenser, but instead of walking back to the table, headed over to the closest table to the entrance—on a path that took him along the chow line.

He slowed down, timing his approach until the sergeant just served by the gladiator thanked her and stepped away. Hondo jumped into the line in front of the next sergeant, almost knocking the tray out of his hands. With the gladiator looming over him, he spun around, facing BK, and raised his glass with one hand and gave a thumbs up with his other.

"No pictures!" a Navy lieutenant commander with the gold shoulder braid of a staff officer shouted, rushing forward to stop him.

BK returned the thumbs up, and Hondo bolted out of the line.

He thought he heard a "Good one, lance corporal," in the deep voice of a gladiator.

Hondo rushed back to his seat as the lieutenant commander shouted out, "No pictures, people. We don't have time. Everyone will get an official holo, but no private pictures."

"Upload it," he told BK as he slid into his seat.

"Already did," she said with a smile. "Hondo, you're my fucking hero."

Chapter 20
Hondo

Hondo ran the rake over the sand, smoothing out the footprints that had been tracked through it. It was after 2300, and the night sky was awash in stars, giving him enough light to keep working.

He heard the crunch, crunch, crunch of steps behind him but didn't bother to look. With another five or six hours to go, he had a long night ahead of him.

"You missed some tracks," the first sergeant's voice reached him.

Hondo straightened his back and turned. The first sergeant was standing in the middle of the patch he'd just raked, his footprints visible in the starlight.

"Sorry, First Sergeant. I'll get that," he said, walking back to rake out the new prints.

He paused, then, the rake motionless beside the first sergeant's boot. With a harrumph, the first sergeant stepped back onto the path, then headed to the SNCO's berthing. Hondo carefully raked out the last three prints, then moved back to where he'd left off.

On the other side of the path, BK worked, raking her section smooth as well. He felt a little guilty about her being there, but she'd insisted that she wasn't upset.

He stood still for a moment, just looking at the sky, his PA burning a hole in his pocket. He couldn't resist. He took it out and opened Connect. In Spot Prime, there he was, a goofy smile on his face while behind him, a surprised-looking CWO5 Curnutte stared right at the camera. BK had let the Connect identifier flag both the gladiator and himself, then added, "Holo by BK Dodds." Already, the post had garnered over a million Love Its, but one meant more than all the rest. As one of the flagged subjects, the gladiator could have had the post deleted, but instead, right at the top of the list, there was her Love It, and the comment, "Semper fi, Devil Dog. Grab what you want in life."

He stared at the image for a moment, then put the PA back in his pocket. Close by, laughter broke out from one of the berthing boxes, Marines relaxing in the night.

In front of him was a large expanse of sand he had to rake smooth, even if it would all be for naught in the morning when Marines trampled over it again. He had a long night ahead of him and all for nothing. Well, not quite for nothing.

It was fucking worth it, he thought as a smile crept over his face.

Chapter 21
Skylar

"It's moving," Sky said to the others at the Kid's Table, as they now referred to themselves.

"We knew it wasn't just going to sit there," Knight said.

Sky ignored him as she watched the holo. Compiled from over a thousand feeds, it provided amazing detail. Currently, they were seeing a view as if hovering 500 meters over the planet's surface, but afterwards, they could rotate, zoom, and adjust the holo as needed to analyze what had happened.

That was the mission, analysis. The Brotherhood soldiers and French Legionnaires might be about to fight for their lives, but hundreds, no, thousands of scientists of all stripes were watching to gauge the effectiveness of the new equipment.

As with K-1003, the UAM command had chosen a world long conquered by the Dictymorphs, one with minimal numbers of the enemy still on it. The military force facing them was a Brotherhood-French brigade, the core being the Brotherhood battalion and French company that had been on K-1003. Both of the original units had been beaten up during the previous battle, but with reinforcements filling in the gaps and an additional two Brotherhood battalions, the brigade had over 3,000 soldiers and Legionnaires, all with taraline up-armored combat suits and the next generation of weapons.

What the brigade didn't have was Klethos unit.

Sky thought that was a mistake. They shouldn't just be testing weapons but also integrated combat. Just at the

Klethos couldn't fight the Dictymorphs alone, neither could humans.

It wasn't up to her, though.

The Legionnaires had advanced almost five kilometers before the Dictymorph seemed to awake. The Legionnaires saw that, too. They spread out into three lines, a hundred meters between each line before they started to run, closing the distance.

At just over two kilometers, the Dictymorph started firing, tendrils of light reaching out to the advancing French—and the company of Legionnaires, 94 strong, started firing back with both their combat suit's internal weaponry as well as several developmental weapons given to them.

"Look at the readings," L'Teesha said. "Degradation is down 52%."

"It would be better with separate shields," Skagt muttered.

Give it a rest.

"What were your projections?" Sky asked L'Teesha.

"I was hoping for 60%, but I'll take 52."

The first of the new particle-tipped missiles exploded on or adjacent to the Dictymorph. Sky looked at the Omega-scan, but there was no decrease of the Dictymorph's output. She hadn't given the missiles much of a chance. They were simply a different method of delivering the energy, and when fired in a particle beam, it hadn't proven effective.

"Lost one Legionnaire," Manny said.

"Two," Wysteria added.

"Load the failure parameters," Sky told them, struggling to keep her voice calm.

The numbers mattered in determining how to improve body armor, but two Legionnaires had just died while they sat safe and sound on Purgamentium.

The holo lit up as more and more weapons were fired, the AI color-coding them for easier comprehension. The Legionnaires kept advancing as more of them fell.

"Body mass down 6%," Sky noted.

It had become evident that the Dictymorphs somehow converted body mass to energy and used that energy as a weapon. By measuring the energy expended and how quickly the mass disappeared, the should be able to determine the efficiency of the process, and thereby know just how many "bullets" were in the Dictymorphs' magazines.

"When do the French stop?" L'Teesha asked.

"You didn't listen?" Skagt asked. "They told us at the brief. Five hundred meters."

L'Teesha rolled her eyes but said nothing.

Fifteen Legionnaires were killed before the first line came to a halt and went flat, followed by the next two lines. Fire intensified as the Dictymorph started advancing on them.

"Here they come," Skagt said, his voice cracking.

Skipping across the ground in what the military called "map of the earth," 108 Brotherhood merkabah, the heavily shielded combat sleds, charged the Dictymorph from behind. Covering the ground at close to 300 KPH, it took them four minutes to close the distance and only two to come within firing range. As the first blast of meson beams hit it, the Dictymorph seemed to hesitate for a moment.

"It's fucking confused," Manny said in awe. "We surprised the shit out of it."

No one knew how to interpret Dictymorph body language, but Sky had to agree that it seemed confused, at least.

The creature convulsed, then it started firing its lights in both directions.

"Total output is the same," Manny said, back on his readouts.

"So, only half is directed to each force," Sky said.

Finally, something concrete.

"Body mass down 13%," she said.

More Legionnaires and now Brotherhood host fell, but at a slower rate. The armor degradation, particularly among the French, was reduced. At initial blush, it looked like there was only so much energy a Dictymorph could expend, and by surrounding it, they had forced it to broaden its sweep, thereby diluting its power.

The Brotherhood soldiers dismounted at 700 meters, having lost twelve sleds, but only 22 men. Most of those who'd been on sleds that had been downed survived to chase after the rest.

It became a battle of attrition, but one that favored the humans. Sky counted down the mass to 80%, 60%, 40%. The Dictymorph was losing mass faster than it was killing humans. And it wasn't just the mass. Several of the weapons were damaging it, particularly the three heat-based weapons.

As a scientist, Sky almost wished they weren't using them. With their added effect on the Dictymorph, that would make the calculation of mass-to-energy that much harder to determine.

Except that would mean more men and women lost, she chided herself.

At 30%, the outcome was a foregone conclusion. Congratulations had begun to be passed among them. Sky watched the numbers fall as the Dictymorph shrunk.

Just as its mass hit 18%, the Dictymorph exploded in a fireball.

"What the hell?" Manny said, voicing everyone else's thoughts.

Sky looked back at the Omega-scan, and the Dictymorph didn't exist anymore. It was simply gone.

As were most of the front-line Legionnaires and twenty more Brotherhood soldiers. No previous Dictymorph had exploded like that. They had simply collapsed like a deflated balloon.

"Did it suicide?" Sky asked, more to herself than to the others.

"Unless it reached a point-of-no-return," Aurora Ricci said.

The physicist had been pushing the idea that the Dictymorphs kept their form with a pool of energy that attracted the cells of the body, sort of an organic gravity. She and Knight Hastert were two of the theory's prime proponents. Sky wasn't so sure about that, and she doubted that if there was such a point, that it would result in an explosion.

"We won," Skagt said, interrupting her thoughts.

Sky looked at him, ready to remind him of how many people had died for his so-called victory, but then it hit her. He was right, not so much as "winning," but in that humans, without Klethos help, had just killed a Dictymorph. Human soldiers, that was. Dictymorphs had been killed by aircraft and Navy ships, and they'd fled humans, but this was the first documented time one had been killed.

The price had been steep, but from the data gathered, the results had been invaluable. Not just in what they'd learned, but in morale. With growing numbers of people protesting human participation in the war, they needed a victory.

They'd just gotten one. The price had been high, but still, it was a victory.

Chapter 22
Hondo

"That should be us there," BK said as they watched the Legionnaires advance.

An image popped into Hondo's mind, a mortally wounded Sam, his head in BK's lap. He shook his head as if he could physically eject the scene from his mind.

"We haven't been upgraded yet, you know that," he said, keeping his voice on an even keel, trying not to let the dread that sometimes overcame him show.

"We've got the taraline already. I know we don't have the rest yet, but still, they got the first victory. It should be us. We've paid in blood for the privilege. Why the Legion first?"

"Because their Rigs already had manual back-ups. Less to do on them."

"Yeah, but . . ." she trailed off.

It had taken awhile after K-1003 for the think tanks to come up with the combat suit modifications. Most of the mods had been related to the taraline surfaces, increasing the shielding the interior circuits within each suit, and to install manual controls and triggers for the more important functions. The Rigaudeau-6's already had many of the manual functions already, so they'd been the first to get the rest of the upgrades. As a result, they'd been sent with the two Brotherhood battalions on the next mission.

And yesterday, they'd killed a Grub. Not make it retreat, but kill it. This morning, all hands on the planet had watched the battle recordings with officers and civilians narrating what had happened.

And it was pretty impressive. When the Grub exploded, the messhall with the 3/6 and 2/14 Marines had erupted into cheers.

That had been tempered when the butcher's bill was tallied. The Legionnaires and Brotherhood had paid dearly for the win, but most of that had resulted from the Grub suiciding.

All four of the fire team Marines were sitting together, but Xeras and Sunrise were focused on the portable holo display that had been set up in the messhall, along with most of the rest of the battalion's non-rates and NCOs. Hondo had thought that they would go back to the day's training after the debrief, but when three more Grubs were spotted, the powers-that-be decided that a real-time view of the battle would be good both as a learning tool and for morale.

"I gotta admit, those Rigs are good-looking suits," BK whispered to Hondo as the current feed showed the Legionnaires advancing in a company column, platoon wedges.

Greater France paid a high percentage of its GDP on its military, a much higher percentage than the Federation did. As a result, even if the Legion was much smaller in number than the Marines, their equipment was top-notch, and that included their Rigaudeau-6's. Sleeker-looking than the Marine PICS, they none-the-less packed some serious muscle.

"Yeah, they look good, but I'll keep our PICS," Hondo said, not wanting to admit the Marines lagged behind anyone in any matter.

"Oh, come on, you mean you wouldn't like to test drive one of those babies?" BK asked.

"I guess. I mean just to see what they're like," Hondo admitted before adding, "Not that I would want to go into combat with one."

"Bullshit."

Hondo didn't bother to respond. She was right.

The holo display shifted to a close-up view of the three targets. The Grubs were arrayed in a three-pointed star, tendrils shooting out 360 degrees.

"Look at that," Hondo said. "The Grubs have adjusted their tactics."

"What do you mean?" BK asked. "So, there's three of them."

The Grubs seemed to be solitary fighters, at least to date. Even the ambush on K-1003 had been more of two Grubs being in the same area rather than working together. BK didn't think much of the fact that there were three in the same place this time, but that wasn't Hondo's point.

"Look at that formation. They can provide mutual support for each other. There's not going to be an envelopment like the Brotherhood did yesterday, I mean if there is one, it won't be as effective."

"Cape buffalo will do the same thing," Sunrise said, almost under her breath.

So, she is listening in—which isn't a bad thing. Still, Cape buffalo don't fly themselves through space using technology we still don't understand.

Just how smart the Grubs were was a hot subject among the humans on the planet, and the junior Marines were no different. Most of the other Marines seemed to consider the Grubs as some sort of large animal, a very dangerous animal, but one acting primarily on instinct. Like the Klethos, they hadn't exhibited much in the way of military arts, but no one was trying to assert that the Klethos were not sentient. From his point of view, Hondo thought any creature that could manage to travel between stars, and without discernable ships, had to have intelligence. Just because they didn't show much in the way of tactics, just because they didn't have rifles and other manufactured weapons, didn't mean they lacked technology. They'd shot down two naval ships, and no one knew how yet.

Hondo turned slightly to include Sunrise in the conversation.

"I don't think they're much like cape buffalo," he said.

"No, I'm just saying that just because the happened into a formation, that doesn't mean they're budding Sun Tzus. It could have been an accident, for all we know."

"True. We don't know. So, the worst thing we can do is underestimate them."

There was a small flash of blue energy from around one of the Grubs that caught the attention of the Marines, but nothing more. The focus died back down as the view changed to one from farther out. The Legionnaires were 15 klicks out and closing, while the Brotherhood soldiers were already mounted on their sleds 30 klicks away.

Marines were taught as a matter of course never to use the same routes while patrolling. Hondo thought the same principles should be followed in battle tactics. The human force was using the same playbook for today's battle as yesterday's.

"How come the Grubs can't see the Legionnaires when they can shoot down spaceships?" Rosy asked from where he and Loren were sitting with their team.

Good question.

In every case so far, but Grubs hadn't commenced firing until the humans or Klethos were between five and six klicks away. But they'd knocked two ships out of orbit. It didn't make sense to him.

BK nudged him with her elbow. She held out half of a pack of Love Nuts, her jaw working on the other half. Hondo held out a hand, and she poured out the rest. Where BK preferred to pop a bunch of them into her mouth at once, Hondo preferred to eat the candy one at a time. He settled back on the bench, eating one after the other while waiting for the battle to develop.

He'd never watched a battle develop in real time before. It was nothing like being in a battle of course, but it was nothing like watching a war flick, either. The real thing would bore most of the audience to tears, he realized.

Until the action really starts.

The Legionnaires slowed down their progress as they approached that six-klick line.

Maybe they are switching things up, Hondo thought. *It doesn't look like they're closing in.*

"I think they're going to stand off," he said.

"Eh, maybe. Makes sense, I guess," she said. "If one of them explodes and sets off the other two, you don't want to be too close."

At seven klicks, the Legionnaires opened fire, missiles, rockets, and backpack mortars reaching for the Grubs. Weaponry rained down on the enemy, and within moments, light spheres rose from the Grub closest to the Legion company.

Only from one, Hondo noted. *The other two aren't firing.*

Love Nuts forgotten, Hondo watched as the spheres rose and approached the Legionnaires, his nervous anticipation rising. Beams of energy weapons, the display coloring each type for easy identification, reached out to the spheres, but still, they advanced. Hondo had heard that the beams were generated by different sources and covered a wide range of frequencies and patterns to see if any would have better effect, but from his perspective, nothing was working. The two spheres reached the company, and light tendrils shot down among the Legionnaires.

The portable display didn't show data such as casualties, but it was obvious that Legionnaires had just died. A mass groan filled the hall as that fact became obvious.

"Here comes the Brotherhood," BK said.

A ragged cheer replaced the groans as the two Brotherhood battalions, one to the east and another to the northwest, went into motion, crossing their LODs.

"Hurry the hell up," Hondo said as the near Grub launched two more spheres.

He couldn't tell how many Legionnaires had fallen, and now the display resolution of the company had been lowered—which was evidence alone that the casualties had been high. With only a few KIA, the brass would have kept the resolution high so everyone could observe what was happening.

The Brotherhood sleds rushed forward, closing the gap. Meanwhile, the Legionnaires were getting pummeled. The commander must have had enough of that because the surviving Legionnaires started to rush forward.

Closing the gap beyond six klicks would open the Legionnaires to the direct light tendrils, but the most effective weapons humans had were the Klethos pikes and perhaps their incendiary devices, all which required them to close in with and engage the enemy. They had no choice if they were going to kill the Grubs.

The remaining two Grubs started launching their own spheres. They intercepted the incoming merkabah sleds, knocking a handful down and out of the fight.

"Shit," someone exclaimed in a muted tone while most of the Marines fell silent as they watched.

Even the captain who'd been giving the commentary had fallen silent as he watched the battle display.

As the human forces closed, the spheres gave way to the tendrils, radiating from them like a tesla ball gone wild. There were no gaps in the tendrils, and if one Grub faltered for an instant, one of the other two filled in the gap.

The humans were having an effect, however. It was obvious to Hondo and the rest that the barrage of incoming fire was hurting them. The question was who was going to blink first.

It was the Grubs.

In unison, the three Grubs broke their formation and darted towards the southwest, trying to break out between the Legionnaires and one of the battalions before the two human forces could link.

A cheer rose up from the Marines, and BK pounded on his shoulder in excitement.

"I knew it!" she shouted. "Look at the bastards run!"

The Grubs were amazingly quick, but the sleds were quicker. They immediately went into pursuit mode, every available weapon firing away. It wouldn't be good enough to force a Grub retreat—the only acceptable conclusion was to have three dead Grubs.

"They're trying for the ravine," Rosy said, looking up from his PA.

Hondo pulled out his, then zooming out from what was on the portable display. It did look like the Grubs were fleeing for a series of ravines that dotted the landscape as if an ancient god had gouged them out with godly claws. The Grubs were pretty big creatures, so Hondo wasn't sure they could lose the humans in the ravines, but it made sense on their part to try. With the lead battalion so close, however, Hondo thought they Grubs might be caught before they could reach cover.

The Marines were shouting their encouragement, and just as it looked like the battalion would catch the three Grubs, they darted forward with previously unseen speed. Only they didn't rush into a ravine, but stayed on the higher ground, surrounded by them.

One of the Grubs gave off a flash of feeble light, then slowed to a halt. Hondo hadn't seen what had hit it, but it wasn't running. The other two kept fleeing for a moment before they turned and came back to the hurt one.

"They can work together," Hondo said.

"Once again, so do cape buffalo," Sunrise said again.

Hondo was not an expert on various wildlife, but he was sure this was not rote instinct. The other two were making a decision based on some sort of thought process, not instinct. It was going to kill them, so it might not be a good decision, but still, it was not simple instinct.

The closest battalion entered the edge of the first ravine, then bent off to the right. It took a moment for Hondo to figure out why. Then it became clear. It was making room for the second battalion so they could surround and pound the three Grubs. The Legionnaires, much slower on foot, was advancing as well, but Hondo figured they'd be late for the party. The battle would be decided before they could get there.

Fire intensified as the players got into position over the next fifteen minutes. With one Grub laying quiet, only two were putting out tendrils, but they were enough to hold the first battalion at bay while the second rushed to join the final firefight. Fire slammed into the Grubs as well, and it was having an effect.

"Look at that shit," BK said as one of the Grub's blue-white tendrils shifted to a more orange-white. "We kicked the blue right out of it."

The scientist-types would have to figure out if orange-white was worse than blue-white, but Hondo agreed with BK that is was probably a good thing.

The second battalion flowed across the flat ground between ravines, pushing past the three Grubs and cutting off any further avenue of retreat. This was going to end, and end now. No more running. The trail battalion slipped into position, and without waiting for the Legionnaires to arrive, the two Brotherhood battalions closed in for the kill.

"This is what I'm talking about," Rosy said, elbow-bumping BK.

Hondo sat silence, ready to simply watch the death dance of the Grubs. He wondered what was going on with their thought process. Were they afraid? Were they complacent?

He was looking right at them when all three erupted in an orgy of light—not an explosion, but controlled light tendrils, just more than they'd show before.

Hondo felt a wave of anxiety sweep over him as the room went silent again.

"It's just a last gasp," BK said, her voice not sounding too sure.

And then the entire display lit up, blinding it out until the compensators kicked in. Hundreds, if not thousands, of tendrils reached out to hit the Brotherhood soldiers—and not just from the three Grubs. Thirty or forty Grubs had risen from the ravines and were now engaged.

"It's an ambush," Hondo said in amazement. "They fucking ambushed us!"

Even watching over a display representation of the battle, Hondo could almost see the hesitation in the Brotherhood forces as they tried to switch up to meet the new threat. Soldiers fell as the unit commanders issued new orders. Within five minutes, at least 40% of the soldiers had fallen, and unit integrity broke down into individuals and small groups struggling to stay alive.

The Legionnaires were closing in to help, but Hondo knew it wouldn't do any good. Soldiers were alive and fighting, but the battle had already been decided. Those were dead men walking out there, and Hondo felt helpless.

A Grub dissipated into nothingness, but no one cheered. They were all too numb.

"The Brotherhood's bringing in their monitor," the captain who'd been giving the commentary said to no one in particular.

Hondo couldn't see that on his PA, but the captain would have access to more data.

I hope it gets there in time.

A monitor was an unmanned or lightly-manned orbiting ship, all big guns and massive amounts of power. Controlled by another command ship, it could destroy ground units or installations without putting a manned ship in danger.

More soldiers fell, and Hondo lost all hope when a bright light-green bolt of energy lit up the display. Light-green was the color assigned by the display AI to indicate naval gunfire. The monitor had spoken.

More than spoken. Three Grubs were incinerated. They simply ceased to exist.

Before the watching Marines could react, though, the three original Grubs, the three that had acted as decoys to suck the humans into the ambush, somehow "converged" their tendrils, which came together above them and formed a single beam that reached into the sky.

Hondo glanced back up at the captain, and when the man swore and flung his PA to the ground, he didn't need to ask what had happened. The three Grubs had shot down the monitor. A moment later, five other Grubs converged their tendrils, sending that beam up as well.

He had no way of knowing, but Hondo was sure the Brotherhood ship that controlled the monitor had been shot down as well.

On the ground, only a few soldiers fought on. Several of the Grubs formed a separate group and headed to the Legionnaires.

The display cut off. Hondo checked his PA, but the feed was cut off there as well. There was no malfunction. The brass had evidently decided that the troops didn't need to see the end unfold.

"Fuck," BK said quietly from beside him.

Yeah, "fuck" is right.

Chapter 23
Skylar

Sky slipped into the seat beside Bill and asked, "Do you know what's going on?"

"Not a clue. Well, considering . . . it has to be related."

Around her, the entire executive and command staff, which had grown to several thousand people, was gathering in the auditorium. Sky had been in meetings non-stop since the disaster on K-2947, trying to make sense of what had happened. She was running on stim-sticks and Joltz, which was holding the despair at bay, but only just so.

Losing close to 3,000 men and women was difficult to fathom, especially when things seemed to be progressing. The Dictymorphs had shown a new side, and accusations were flying as to how any of them, and perhaps the Dictymorph team, in particular, had been so wrong.

"So, are you still talking to me?" she asked, watching to see his expression as he answered.

He sighed, tilted his head back, eyes closed, and said, "Yes, I'm still talking to you. It wasn't your fault."

"That's not what most of you military types are saying. Bishop-Colonel West, he's been asking for all of us to be fired, you know. Called us murderers."

"It's his ass on the line. He's the senior Brotherhood military rep. He's got to blame someone." He paused for a second, then opened his eyes and looked at her before continuing, "Do you blame yourself?"

"No . . . yeah. I don't know. I mean, we've been pretty wrong so far. No one thought the Dictymorphs had that degree of adaptability."

"Seems to me you did. At least, you told me that too many were underestimating the Grubs."

"Yeah, to a degree, maybe I was. But not to this extent. And even if I did, I let Janus and the rest set the tone."

"Is it true what I heard about him?"

"Yep. He resigned yesterday. He's on his way back to the Alliance."

Bill shrugged, then said, "Probably a good thing. So, who's taking over his spot? You?"

"Hah! Fat chance of that. I'm not much of a team player. Hastert, maybe, God help us. Possibly L'Teesha."

"L'Teesha?"

"You met her at the Baiae. Turquoise and pink mohawk?"

"Her? She barely speaks."

"She's brilliant, but yeah, she's not much one for talking. Hell, who knows? They may bring in someone new. It's not like no one else is working on this. We're just the advance party. Maybe Gentle Bosovitch. He's had lots of input."

"Oh, here comes the bossman," Bill said, pointing up to the stage where the archbishop and EC Baker were crossing.

Archbishop Lowery reached the middle of the stage and stopped, looking over the people. Three-thousand sets of eyes focused on him.

"In view of our losses on K-2947 . . ." he started before trailing off. "No, not in view of that. I have to be honest with you. This has been building for awhile." He waited again, as if trying to carefully choose his words. "There's really no other way to put it than to be blunt. As of approximately 45 minutes ago, the Brotherhood of Man, the Alliance of Free States, the

Freedom Alliance, and the Denton Stations are withdrawing support from the task force."

There was an audible intake of air as 3000 sets of lungs gasped in shock.

"Not only that, but those governments are petitioning the UAM to cease and desist all operations against the Dictymorphs."

"Holy shit," Bill muttered under his breath.

Stop the fight? What?

"With that in mind, starting immediately, all Brotherhood, Alliance, Freedom Alliance, and Dentonians will begin their immediate recall. Please check with your group admin to get your schedules.

"There's one more thing. This includes all UAM personnel from those governments. Whether you will keep your positions with the UAM is yet to be seen, but you are no longer to contribute to the war effort.

"I have tendered my resignation and have turned over command of the task force to Executive Counsellor Baker who will act as the interim commander."

He paused for a moment, then said, "None of this is a denunciation of the job all of you have done, nor does it negate the sacrifice so many have made. All of you should be proud."

He turned to the EC and simply said, "Terrence?" before walking off the stage.

"Everyone else, please remain seated," the EC said.

The gathered people looked around at each other, not knowing what to do. In fits and starts, individuals stood up and started making their way out of the auditorium. It took four or five minutes for those who were leaving to exit the building.

"I know this is a shock for all of us. It has been a pleasure to work with the archbishop, just as it has been working with all of the colleagues we've come to know. But regardless of whether our ranks have been cut, we still have a mission to fulfill. The Dictymorphs are still out there, and if we don't assist the Klethos, pretty soon we'll be facing them alone.

"All of you, get back to your job sites, get back to training your troops. There'll undoubtedly be some shakeups, but deal with those as they come."

EC Baker walked off the stage despite the hands shooting up by people with questions.

Sky had questions, too. Many of them. Perhaps the most pressing one, however, seemed to have been forgotten. It was one thing for the EC to tell them to all soldier on, but how were the Klethos going to take the news?

Chapter 24
Hondo

First Squad stood silently, watching the lines of Brotherhood soldiers load their shuttles down on the spacepad. Yesterday, there had been some 20,000 of them on the planet. By tomorrow, they would all be gone.

"Fucking cowards," BK said.

Within that same day, the soldiers had gone from respected brothers in arms given condolences for losing two battalions to being vermin. Hondo knew it wasn't the individual soldier's fault, but he couldn't help feeling disdain. It was as if once they got their nose bloodied, they ran. It had well over a hundred years since the Brotherhood host had done any serious fighting, and he was beginning to wonder if their vaulted strength was a mirage.

Beyond the shuttles, another small craft stood, representing something far different. The 20-passenger reconnaissance craft, able to fly through bubble space as well as land on a planet, belonged to the Greater French Navy. As soon as the shuttles lifted off, the ship, with 15 Legion commandos on board, would return to K-2947. One of the satellites still orbiting the planet had picked up a distress sign. Four Legionnaires, without any powered equipment, and left a simple SOS and message made out of rocks, hoping it would be spotted. Admiral Lopez had offered the Legion full assistance, but the Legion said they take care of their own.

The Legion and the Marines had clashed a number of times over the years, but at that moment, Hondo felt a kinship with them. More than that, he respected them.

Jonathan P. Brazee

"Well, Soldier," Sergeant Mbangwa said as he stepped up beside him. "All that means is that only the best will be left here."

"You got that right, Sergeant," he replied. "We don't need them."

Except, he knew they did need them. All of humanity had to be dedicated to the cause if they were going to succeed. He knew that, but he didn't want to admit that as he watched the host leave.

The sergeant said, "OK, enough gawking. Let's get back to camp."

As they started off again, BK asked, "Hondo, how come the sergeant always calls you "Soldier." We're Marines, not soldiers. I've always wanted to ask you that."

"Yeah, me too, Rosy said. "It's kinda weird. He calls everyone else by our names, even me."

The sergeant was probably the only one to call Rosy "Roosevelt." Most sergeants used last names and ranks for the non-rates, but when not giving actual orders, he often reverted to first names.

"Because that's my name," he said, stepping off in trace of their squad leader.

"No, hold on. You can't leave it at that," BK said, hurrying to reach his side. "That's not your name."

Hondo had never been too forthcoming about his past. He wasn't ashamed of it, but it was nothing to trumpet about, either. But these were his friends.

"My name means "soldier" in Shona. So, he calls me that," he admitted.

"'Soldier in Shona?'" she asked. "I know you're from Paradhiso, but you . . ."

"But I don't look like the sergeant, right? I've got freakin' freckles across my nose, right? Don't you think I've heard that enough times in my life growing up?" he asked with more venom in his voice than he'd intended.

"Shit, don't snap off my head, Hondo. Or should I say, Soldier?"

"Sorry, I didn't mean that. Look, I may not be a Black Blood like the sergeant, but I'm still Shona."

"Black Blood?"

"Part of the royal family. A *Youmambo*. The current *mambo* may be only an honorary figurehead, but the Black Bloods still run the planet and own most of it."

"And the sergeant is a prince or something?" Rosy asked.

"Yeah, something like that."

"Hell, yeah. I may have to go visit him there when all of this is done," he said, a big smile on his face.

"So, I take it you weren't from one of the upper classes?"

"Again, you can say that."

They walked on for another 100 meters when she said, "Still, royal blood or not, the sergeant seems like a good bloke. He treats you better than the rest of us, in fact. I'm not complaining, just observing."

"Some Black Bloods are privileged assholes, BK, always taking, never giving. Not the sergeant. He's got to be worth a mint, and he's got his choice of high-level positions for him if he'd go home, but he reenlists for the Corps? As only a sergeant, not an officer even? And he's never cut me down for my *imbwa muko* accent. No, he's one of the good ones."

"Imbwa what?"

"It's slang, kind of meaning "dog boy," but not in proper Shona.

"So, if you put that together, you're kind of a Dog Soldier, right? That's a proud title, you know."

"A what?"

"A Dog Soldier. The elite warriors of the Cheyenne Nation."

"The Cheyenne? The native Americans?"

"Damned right. Wicked fearsome, you know."

Hondo looked at her in surprise. He'd never heard her spout off facts like that.

BK saw the expression on his face, and a scowl crossed hers. "Hey, I'm not ignorant. I can read me some fucking history, too."

She sped up, pulling ahead of him.

"Nice move, Soldier," Rosy said. "Pissed her but real."

"Eat me, *Roosevelt*."

But Rosy was right. He shouldn't have acted so surprised that BK had studied something other than the latest immersion game. He could tell that hurt her.

Dog Soldiers. I'm going to have to look them up.

He looked back over his shoulder one more time at the spacepad and the Brotherhood host loading up, then put them out of his mind and followed his squad leader.

They still had a war to win.

Chapter 25
Hondo

Corporal Yetter stared into Hondo's eyes as if trying to dig down into his soul. Hondo kept his own eyes blank, focusing five meters beyond his fellow team leader. With a sudden, vicious punch, Yetter hit Hondo in his right bicep, almost driving him to his knees.

Hondo's vision tunneled for a moment, and he felt more than saw Yetter turn him sideways before smashing his knee into Hondo's thigh.

He barely stayed on his feet. He didn't have to look to see his thigh was a mass of bruised flesh. He took two deep breaths, then stood straighter, not quite in a drill field position of attention, but about the best he could do, considering. Corporal Yetter simply nodded, then stepped back.

Sergeant Mbangwa stood up and almost sauntered over, his entire body screaming lethality. Hondo's vision returned, and this time, he didn't stare off somewhere beyond the man but right into his eyes. He wanted to see his fate coming for him.

Aside from being a *Youmambo,* aside from being rich, handsome as all get out, and a hell of a Marine, the sergeant was a beast, muscles bulging under his t-shirt. Hondo couldn't help but swallow nervously as the sergeant approached.

Maybe he'll go light on me? Hondo wondered. *Viva Paradhiso and all?*

The sergeant stood in front of Hondo for a moment, a menacing threat, and in an instant, Hondo knew the sergeant was not going to take it easy on him. If anything, he was going to go into beast mode.

"You ready, Soldier?"

Hondo nodded.

"On three, then. One . . ."

On "two," the sergeant straight-punched Hondo's shoulder, knocking him completely off his feet. The other NCO's hooted and hollered their appreciation.

Someone, maybe Yetter, maybe someone else, grabbed Hondo by his left arm, but the sergeant said, "No, make him get up on his own."

Hondo was nauseous, and he felt like he was going throw up, a bit of pre-vomit rising to his mouth, gastric juices burning his throat.

I'm not going to puke, he told himself, manfully swallowing the mouthful that had come up.

He got to his feet, stumbling only once, and drew himself erect in front of his sergeant. His body trembled as Mbangwa turned him 90 degrees. This time, there was no playing around. Sergeant Mbangwa kneed his thigh, collapsing the leg. Somehow, Hondo managed to stay at least half-up, his left leg trembling.

Sergeant Mbangwa watched as Hondo straightened and stood fully erect.

He looked over the rest of the Marines and corpsmen, then announced, "I welcome Corporal Hondo McKeever into the ranks of Marine non-commissioned officers. Let no senior doubt his determination, let all juniors fear his wrath!"

There was a cheer as the rest of the platoon's corporals, sergeants, and the two HM3 corpsmen cheered, men and women who'd all just beat the living crap out of him.

"*Makorokoto*, Soldier," the sergeant said as he helped Hondo take a seat. "Took it like a real Marine."

"Hey, you corporals, what's the matter with you? Give your newest E4 a beer!" he shouted, hand still on Hondo's shoulder.

Corporal Yetter—*Paul* to him now—rushed up with a cold Ariel from the case someone had swiped or traded for from the Confeds. Hondo didn't want it, afraid of the nausea that still roiled his stomach, but this was part of the tradition as well.

An illegal tradition.

Getting his rank "pounded" was considered hazing, and that was specifically prohibited by the UFCMJ. That was one of the traditions, along with recon "blood wings," that was routinely ignored by the brass. A lance corporal was promoted to E4, usually by the company commander. But he or she was not considered part of the NCO mafia until the chevrons were pounded into the shoulder and the "blood stripe" was kneed into the thigh.

After the party broke up, Doc Pataki would escort him to sickbay to treat him for "falling down." No one, including the battalion surgeon, would bat an eye. A few hours in regen, and he'd be functional, at least, and well on his way to a full recovery.

Using his left arm, Hondo took a swig of the cold ale, and to his surprise, it settled his stomach. He looked up at the rest of the NCO, aware that he'd become one of the true backbones of the modern Marine Corps. Officers did their thing, even SNCOs, but it was the corporals and the sergeants who led Marines into battle.

His arm was throbbing, unable even to hold the beer. He could feel his thigh swelling, but he almost savored the pain for what it represented to him.

He was now an NCO of Marines!

Chapter 26
Skylar

"See, look at the readouts," Christoff said, placing plastisheets in front of each of them. "The data is pretty clear."

Dr. Christoff Hans was one of their replacements, a "newbie," as the military side of the house called them. A structural engineer, he'd managed to pull out a string of data, which if true, could have significant ramifications.

Sky had some doubts about it. The AI's had poured over the same data inputs, as had some of humanity's brightest minds. Still, it was possible. Sky pulled the sheet closer and began to analyze the data from his perspective.

He could be right, she realized as she began to take it in.

She downloaded the data into her PA and ran it through several spin-cycles, and while each of the results differed slightly, they generally ran true. Whether his final theory held water as left to determine, but at least she couldn't disapprove it based on the data.

Christoff's data showed two interlocking factors that seemed to relate to a weapon's, if not efficacy, then ability to impact on the Dictymorphs: speed of the weapon and ambient temperature.

Given the fact that a Klethos pike and even a thrown incendiary device could impact on the body of a Dictymorph, the speed of the weapon or projectile had already been analyzed to death without any obvious correlation. What Christoff postulated was that there was another factor, ambient temperature. At higher temperatures, either ambient or from the warhead itself, more could penetrate the Dictymorph's shielding.

But he didn't stop there. He also threw in a monkey wrench. Some missiles, such as a Marine M48, initially were able to penetrate the shielding, even if they had no discernable effect on the Dictymorphs, but lost that ability even at higher ambient temperatures. According to Christoff, the answer was simple. The Dictymorphs were adjusting the settings, so to speak, of their shielding. They'd lowered the barrier to a slower speed, hence blocking out those weapons.

Hell, not "he could be right." I think he is right.

That was one of the problems with human society, the reliance on AIs. AIs could navigate faster, fire weapons more accurately, churn through huge amounts of data, and do many things better than humans could. What they took a back seat to humans, however, was in intuition.

Warhead speed and temperature had been examined, but as those two alone didn't fit the ground truth, they were discarded. Christoff, brand new to the team and so with a new set of eyes, had keyed onto an overlooked factor: Dictymorph ability to adjust to meet conditions.

It was pretty embarrassing. They all knew the Dictymorphs were not static entities. The battle on K-2947 had proven that. Why hadn't anyone previously considered that factor?

No time for recriminations now. If this pans out, we can outfit the Marines and soldiers with much more effective weapons.

And that meant fewer human and Klethos deaths.

Chapter 27
Hondo

"Shift right, Xeras. I don't think Dodds wants you to light up her ass," Hondo passed on the fire team net.

In the front of the wedge, BK turned around and spotted Xeras. Their P2P telltale lit off, and while Hondo couldn't listen in, he could imagine BK blistering her hide. It was all well and good to let AI governors handle the problem of friendly fire, but couple the potential for having their power cut with the fact that some of the new weapons had not been integrated into the suits yet, well, BK was right to worry.

He looked down at his new grappling hook. When he'd told Sam and BK about General Lysander earning his Nova by killing a Capy with a grappling hook, he'd never thought he'd be outfitted with one.

Not that it was a real grappling hook. It just looked like one, and the Marines had taken to referring to them as such. With the fans folded against the side of the shaft at the moment, it was light and easy to maneuver. Once it hit a Grub, however, and the tip penetrated its body, the fans would shoot out, and the current, based on the same principle as the Klethos pikes, would deploy. The idea was that with the fans deployed inside the body, it would be difficult for the Grubs to pull them out.

And of particular interest to the Marines, the hook could be deployed from a distance. If they worked, there wouldn't be a requirement to close in to hand-to-Grub combat as with the pikes.

In keeping with the whole loss of power thing, the head of the hooks could be fired either under PICS power or mechanically. Using the PICS, the hook could reach 100 meters. If a PICS lost power, with a lot of sweat expended, a Marine could employ it by mechanical means.

"Keep moving, BK," Hondo reminded her.

She turned and continued forward, closing in on the target.

With Paul on his fire team to his right and Dixie Freemechman and her team on his left, the squad advanced on line. Everything looked good, so, of course, that was when they were hit.

Sergeant Mbangwa's avatar grayed out.

Oh, shit!

Immediately, command passed to Dixie as the senior corporal.

"Keep advancing, and guide on me."

As the center fire team in an otherwise featureless approach, the squad had been guiding on First Fire Team. Hondo didn't understand why she changed it, but she was the boss. And that meant the Xeras, on the left side of the wedge, had the responsibility to guide off of Third Fire team now.

For a moment, Hondo considered switching to a V, which would shift that responsibility to BK, but only for a moment. Xeras had to learn.

"Heads up. Report any movement to me," Dixie passed to the squad.

Calm down, Dix. We know what to do.

"Private Xeras, I said guide on Second. You're too far forward.

Sergeant Mbangwa was not a micromanager, never telling someone what to do just to hear his own voice. And he'd never given a tactical order directly to a rifleman, as far as

Hondo knew. Dixie was not as assured, however, and she tended to micro-manage things.

"Hey, Dixie. Let me know if you need us to adjust. I'll take care of Xeras."

"You weren't, so I stepped in," she said curtly before cutting the circuit.

Hondo rolled his eyes. She was nervous, he could see, so he'd just go with the flow for now.

"Targets in sight," Rosy passed on the squad net. "Three, I repeat, three, Grubs in a line, 700 meters at zero-five-five."

"Keep up the advance," Dixie passed. "Unit integrity."

The squad passed the slight rise, and then Hondo could see the three "Grubs" as well. These weren't the DreamWorks automatons, which were far too valuable to be simple targets. The Grubs were shipping crates covered with white tarps. They were cheap, but they didn't move and had to be replaced after each engagement.

A light flashed beside one the Grubs.

"Check your shield strengths," Dixie passed. "Speed to three-five-kay-pee-aich."

Immediately, the twelve remaining Marines, along with Doc Pataki, stepped up their cadence. Within moments, all thirteen of them were loping forward at the sustained speed. Hondo might have gone into superman mode, regardless of the slight weakening of their shield power, but with the taraline up-armor, they now had almost 30 seconds of breathing room before the shields would fail.

At least, that's what the civilians promised.

The light sphere "hit," and immediately Rosy and Private Hortense-Realto were taken out.

"Keep going," Dixie passed.

The remainder of the squad closed the distance. At 150 meters, Hondo raised his hook, ready to fire. At 105 meters, his power went out.

"Son-of-a-bitch," he shouted, his voice going nowhere.

The PICS now had a gyro system that brought the suit to a standing halt once power was lost. Hondo quickly reached up and cranked the display shield. Ten seconds later, he had full view to the front. No one was still advancing, at least that he could see, so everyone must have lost power along with him.

He checked his left arm, which he'd been about to raise when the power was cut. It wasn't on target, but it wasn't far off, either. With both hands, now, he turned the wheels that gave vertical and horizontal motion. Cranking both and getting out of breath, he brought the little nub that acted as a crude iron sight, into alignment with the nearest Grub.

He flipped the selector lever and started cranking again, but the latch didn't catch the string. Flipping the selector lever three or four times, he finally got it to catch and started cranking back the string, letting it fall into the tiny groove behind the hook quarrel.

Sweat was dripping off his forehead with the exertion (and lack of working climate control in the suit) as he reached for the left arm trigger release. A burst of flames reached out from his left, enveloping the left Grub. His target, though, was the center Grub. He released the trigger.

Using the mechanical launcher was not as uniform as firing under power. The tension on the string, its position as it fell into the slot, and the position of the hook quarrel all had an effect. With a vibration that Hondo felt through his dead suit, the hook took off.

For a moment, Hondo thought it was going to fall short, but it carried just enough to reach the base of the Grub, bouncing once before hitting it.

Over the next minute, a few more hooks shot out, a few more flames. Some hit, some didn't. The Grub on the right looked almost untouched.

Power flowed back into his PICS. His suit went through its field protocol, and ten seconds later, it was fully functional.

"All hands return to the bleachers," the range operator passed.

"At the double-time," Sergeant Mbangwa said.

"He sounds pissed," Paul passed on the P2P as the Marines started to run back down the length of the range.

"Wouldn't you be? Getting killed before we really started?" Hondo said.

By the time that got back to the bleachers, the sergeant was standing to the side, waiting. If a Marine in a PICS could display anger, then this was the case. Maybe it was the slight tilt at the waist that let him imagine the angry sergeant inside.

If he was angry, he didn't let his voice show it as they gathered around.

"Wait for our debrief," was all he said.

Getting out of the bleachers was a squad of Klethos. Since the fighting forces had been segregated, Hondo had minimal contact with their allies. It was only as they approached the range LOD that he noticed all of them had grappling hooks and launchers as well. They looked no different than the Marines' hooks.

"Look at that," he passed to BK. "We use their tech for the head, but our tech to get it there."

"Beats using the pikes," was all she said.

The Klethos did an abbreviated haka, stomping around and thrusting their grappling hooks into the air. The Marines all watched the dance for a moment. Without a discernable signal, they all wheeled almost in unison and took off down the range.

Hondo would have liked to follow them and observe their attack. He had a feeling in his gut that humans and Klethos would have to work much closer together if they were going to defeat the threat.

Chapter 28
Skylar

Skylar was numb, her body in rebellion from just about every stimulant known to man. At the same time, she was hyped beyond belief. This was it, the first real strike against the Dictymorphs.

She just hoped they'd provided the task force with the tools to win.

Operation Brave Justice had been in the works for two weeks, not nearly enough time for something of this magnitude. Sometimes, though, the enemy doesn't give enough time for long-term planning. When the Klethos liaison had informed the UAM command that the Dictymorphs had invaded one of their planets, one with a large Klethos population, the task force had to take action.

It wasn't as if they'd started from point zero, after all. Everything over the last year had pointed to this. The initial confrontations, the weapons research, the psychological profiling, all had been in preparation for this.

Sky understood the the political ramifications as well, both for the Klethos and for humanity. The Klethos had been patient with the work-ups, but they had to see that humans would do more than hit the Dictymorphs on worlds they had largely abandoned. But this was also a message to the rest of humanity. After the Brotherhood and its faction had pulled out of the task force, more and more opposition to the war had surfaced. The UAM needed a win, and in a big way, to shore up support.

She also understood the risk. A defeat, particularly a catastrophic defeat, could shut down all support.

L'Teesha stepped up behind her and wrapped her arms around Sky's shoulders. "We've done all we can, Sky. Now it's up to them."

"But did we do enough? Just look at them. How many won't return?"

"God knows, men wait to find out."

The two watched the spacepad where thousands of Marines and soldiers were still loading the shuttles. Bill said it would take 18 hours for the entire task force to be aboard the ships and on their way.

She felt a wave of concern. Bill was going on the operation as well. Sky didn't know many on the military side, and none as well as she knew Bill. She didn't want to think about losing him.

Thirty-thousand Marines, soldiers, Legionnaires, and militia were on their way to fight far beyond human space. Four Klethos battalions were in the task force as well, but unlike the humans, they'd be going to a Klethos world. For all she knew, some of them might have been born on K-3363.

This wasn't the Klethos' homeworld. The planet was now populated by the Klethos-lee, but Diane had told them it had once been the home of another species. The Klethos had defeated them and taken over the planet. When asked, she'd told them that the original occupants no longer existed.

For all the Klethos on Purgamentium seemed to be "civilized," Diane's casual comment reflected on the true nature of the Klethos. They'd conducted genocide on 17 different species of intelligent life. Sky liked the Klethos, such as they were, but sometimes even she wondered if they were doing the right thing in supporting them.

"You going to get some sleep?" L'Teesha asked.

"Not just yet. I want to watch them finish the embarkation."

"Remember what they told us. Our bodies need to recover from all the stims, and Procounsel Bari wants all of us ready to go for the landing."

"I know, I know. And I'll get some sleep later."

"Don't wait too long, Sky, OK?"

Sky patted L'Teesha's arm as her friend pulled away. L'Teesha took a step to leave, then stopped and turned back.

"It sucks that you weren't made Chief Xenologist, but all of us at the Kid's Table, we know what you've done. No one could have done better. You've given those young men and women their best shot at coming back home."

Sky looked up in surprise. Yes, she'd been disappointed that she hadn't moved up to Chief Xenologist, but she'd managed to suppress that and focus on the mission. She wasn't an expert in most of the specific disciplines, but she'd like to have thought that she's been a good conduit for the interchange of ideas and courses of action. It touched her that L'Teesha thought she'd been vital to that mission.

A tear formed in the corner of her eye, one she quickly brushed away.

Damned stims, making me all emotional.

She settled back to watch the rest of soldiers go off to war.

K-3363

Chapter 29
Hondo

The shuttle zigged-and-zagged to the surface, slamming the Marines in their cradles. No shuttles had been shot down yet by the Grubs, but they'd proven before that they were willing to try new approaches.

This was to be the real deal, not a test run. Operation Brave Justice was in full swing. Over 30,000 human soldiers and four battalions of Klethos were arriving to reinforce the Klethos already on-planet in an attempt to stop the Grubs from taking it.

Federation Marine recon had already been inserted on the planet, using their clandestine duck eggs, for a week now. They were sending a stream of intel back to Purgamentium and Brussels, and that intel was the basis of the current battle plan.

The Klethos on the planet had been steadily losing ground since the Grub invasion. They didn't have the human fascination with numbers, so no one knew exactly how much of the planetary force still survived. It had taken tremendous casualties, though, that much was evident.

The Joint Klethos-Human Command was going to land in a broad plain down which the Grubs were advancing. The human force was spearheaded by the Federation Marines and Confederation Army, with all other participating governments' military in the force as well, even if with smaller numbers. The Klethos force was four full battalions.

Everybody's got to play for political reasons, Hondo and the rest of the force understood.

They were going in heavy. M2 Mannerheims, the Marine Corps' heavy tanks, had been upgraded with new weapons, weapons designed to kill Grubs. The tanks would form the key defense of the attempt to defend the Klethos city that stood in the way of the Grubs. Arty had been modified, and a fleet of combat drones replaced human-powered aircraft.

The grunts, at Camp Casey, hadn't been aware of the enhancements made to the other branches, and their appearance had been a welcomed surprise. The "Mannies," in particular, looked menacing. There had always been somewhat of a rivalry between PICS Marines and tankers, but Hondo felt better with the tank battalion in the operation.

The shuttle went into its death dive, swooping down at its threshold Gs as it came in for a landing. Hondo tried to keep in his "Battle Meal," the last real food he'd probably eat before the end of the battle, from coming back up his throat.

For some, it would be the last real food they'd *ever* eat.

With a gentle landing at odds with the herky-jeky approach, the shuttle touched down. Hondo hit the release, and the clamps holding him captive opened, setting him free. The 64 Marines ran out the back ramp, already moving to the assembly area. Staff Sergeant Aster, right on Hondo's ass and the last man to debark, had barely jumped off the edge of the ramp before the shuttle lifted off and shot into the air, ready to pick up the next load.

The initial thrust was designed to achieve a rapid build-up of force, getting all hands on the planet surface as quickly as possible. The Klethos, with their personal transport systems, had come in a huge wave, then set up security to allow the humans, with their larger shuttles, to land safely.

The first time they'd attempted this during training six months prior, it had been a goat rope. As usual, unit discipline seemed to be a foreign concept to the Klethos. It had taken rehearsal after rehearsal to work out the kinks—which was ironic in that for the actual operation, where rehearsals were vital, the landing had not been practiced.

Hondo checked his display as the platoon ran to their positions. Each Klethos has been given a repeater that could be picked up by the human battle AIs, and to his welcome surprise, all four Klethos battalions looked to be where they were supposed to be. The Marines were to fall into the Klethos' positions, freeing them up to push farther up the valley and closer to the current battle in this part of the planet.

Kilo Company settled in to wait for the rest of the force, all sensors arrayed forward and combat drones overflying the Line of Advance. With the Klethos between them and the Grubs, the Marines felt somewhat secure, but the Grubs had a habit of defeating human sensors. It would not have surprised anyone had a swarm of Grubs appeared from underground tunnels and attacked them. There was no such attack, though, and four hours later, the last of the initial assault force had landed. Fifteen minutes after the last shuttle took off, the two Klethos battalions co-located with the Marines were given the order to advance immediately followed by the lead Marine battalions. Twenty-eight klicks away, two more Klethos battalions, followed by the Confederation-heavy envelopment force, advanced on a roughly parallel course. Between the two forces, along the high ground, a new Budapest Ranger battalion and a Legion company kept pace with the two larger human units, acting as both a linking and a ready reaction force.

"Keep it calm, Marines. We've got a long ways to go," Sergeant Mbangwa passed on the squad circuit before switching to the three fire team leaders.

"Everyone's hyped up, but we're probably ten hours until contact, and we don't want to shoot our loads now. Xeras and Knight are burning up nervous energy, so try and keep them on an even keel."

Hondo pulled up Xeras' bios. The sergeant was right. Pulse at 120, blood pressure 140 over 100, she was too amped. That would wear her out. He was embarrassed that the sergeant had to not-so-subtly remind him to watch his team better.

"Fiona, you doing OK?" he asked her on the P2P."

"Ready to kick from Grub ass, Corporal," she replied quickly.

"I know you are, but we're at least ten hours to contact, so relax a bit."

"Unless those fuckers surprise us like they did with the Brotherhood," she said.

Which was true. But he still needed to calm her down.

"I'm not saying go take a nap. Keep on the alert, but remember, we've got a Kluck battalion between them and us. We'll have plenty of warning."

Leading Marines could straddle a fine line. They all needed to be alert and ready for anything, but they couldn't wear themselves out before the battle commenced. Hondo almost wished he was back as the AR-man, only concerned about his specific job.

Almost, that was. He wasn't about to give up his corporal's stripes and fire team.

The next nine hours went by uneventfully. Hondo kept up an easy pace, his PICS doing 99% of the work. He ate "ghost shit" to keep his body fueled, and he made use of the gel diapers that kept himself clean. His mind started wandering several times, and he had to snap himself back. Relaxing was all well and good, but they were in a combat zone, and anything could happen.

"Why didn't they just drop us off closer?" Valúlfur had asked seven hours into the march.

"You were there, Sunrise. We needed to keep the shuttles safe to make sure we all got on the ground safely," BK said.

"But look at his empty shit. No Grubs so far."

"And they can shoot down Navy ships," Hondo reminded her. "Who knows what their range is?"

That had been the crux of the matter. No one knew just how far they could range with their weapons. Hondo wondered if the powers that be simply pulled out the distance from their asses.

Two hundred klicks. Sound good to you, Doctor?

I'm certain that is fine, Doctor.

The problem with that was that the science types were back on Purgamentium, safe and sound. If they'd been wrong, Marines—or their body parts—would have been scattered all over the countryside as the shuttles were shot down.

OK, so it didn't happen, he had to admit. *But it could have.*

After they passed nine hours on the march, Captain Montgomery passed, "We're about to enter the city. Remember the ops order. Do not interact with the Klethos there. We're simply passing through."

About a third of the Marines were going to advance through the city to get to the series of strong points that were going to form the basis of the defense in depth. Hondo was glad that 3/6 was to be among that number. Everyone was curious as to what the rest of the Klethos looked like, what their buildings looked like. Two science-types who'd served in the Marines had been put in PICS and were traveling with

Captain Montgomery and Captain Lyle-Quisenberry, the Lima Company commander, loaded for bear with cams and other scanners to gather as much information about the Klethos civilians as they passed through.

As they crested a rise, the city lay sprawled out below them, looking like . . . any other city Hondo had ever seen. There wasn't much in the way of spectacular skyscrapers, and beyond that, the buildings looked rather normal. Within ten minutes at their PICS' trotting speed, they were entering the outskirts. Klethos warriors were lining the roads through which the Marines were to pass. Hondo got the impression that they were there to protect their people from the Marines.

So much for trust among the allies.

They couldn't hide their people, though. Along the road, smaller Klethos with more colors in their neck crests came up to watch them jog by. Without any of the Klethos warriors' armor, they looked far more alien, far more bird-like, than the warriors he was used to. He knew some of them were males, but not how many.

"Oh, eyes right at zero-seven-zero. Baby Klucks," BK said.

Hondo turned and saw at least a dozen of the mini-Klethos. They sure looked like young ones and not simply smaller adults. Two of the warriors, as if aware of the Marines' gazes to the little ones, crowded closer together as if to block the view with their bodies.

"Remember, we're supposed to be looking at the layout in case we have to fall back and defend this place house-to-house," he reminded his three Marines.

It was difficult, though, to ignore the Klethos civilians, when the buildings did not offer very much in the way of the exotic. On closer look, they did have differences from typical human buildings, but those differences were surprisingly few. The windows were sort of lopsided and irregular, there were what looked like little shelves protruding from the outside walls, and what had to be doors looked like they went into the ground instead of opening at street-level.

They passed hundreds of the one-story buildings, then even more multi-story buildings.

"How many do you think live here?" BK asked him.

Hondo had been trying to get a feel for it. On a human world, when faced with imminent danger, the population would have fled, but everywhere he looked, the non-warrior Klethos seemed to be milling about, more curious about the humans than afraid of the advancing Grubs—that is if he was reading them correctly. For all he knew, their demeanor could be a reflection of abject panic.

"I'm guessing close to a million. But we don't know how many of them live in each building. Could be one each or twenty in each one."

"Still, that's a lot of Klucks."

"Hell, we've got cities with a hundred million. This planet doesn't seem that populated."

"So, why are we here, then? Just get the civvy-Klucks out of here and leave the place to the Grubs."

"We've got to make a stand somewhere. This place is as good as any, I'm guessing," Hondo said. "So, enough chatter. Keep an eye out and try to get a feel for this place. We could be back here soon depending on how things work out up ahead."

Fifteen minutes later, they were leaving the city and proceeding to "up ahead," only thirty more klicks away. That was where the Klethos-human force was going to draw their line in the sand.

No one knew if they were going to be able to keep the Grubs from crossing it.

Chapter 30
Hondo

Fifteen hours later, the joint force was still in position, waiting for the Grubs. Perhaps the major advantage of the defense is that the defenders get to select the terrain. However, that means nothing if the attackers choose not to play. If defending the Klethos city behind them was the actual objective, then things were going well. However, the real mission was to close with and destroy the enemy, to validate all the work and effort over the last year-and-a-half.

The Grubs, 206 of them in all, had stopped their advance some 40 klicks from the force's front lines. Several sorties of the planetary-based Klethos had hit the Grubs and been destroyed while accounting for two Grubs, and still, the enemy just sat there, doing nothing.

Hondo could imagine what was going on at the command levels. They had to be shitting bricks, wondering what was happening. In a human war, something would have broken by now, and a good chance that would have been for the defending force, which far outnumbered the attackers, to transition into the assault.

"Second Platoon, just giving you all another head's up," Lieutenant Silas passed, just as she'd done at the top of the last ten hours. "Nothing much has changed with the local Grubs. They've not moved, nor have they expended any energy that we can pick up. However, we do have a bit more information on the rest of the Grubs on the planet. It seems as if all of them have stopped moving. We don't know if they're all communicating somehow or not or what's going on.

"On the friendly side, Task Force Pompeii has shifted closer to the high ground to be ready to close in if and when the Grubs advance to contact."

That bit about the other Grubs, which Intel thought might number over 10,000, having also stopped, was pretty interesting. No one knew just how quickly they could move themselves, and several hundred more of them were within a thousand klicks of the city. Their current Ops order called for a quick extract should any significant number of new Grubs head their way, but that left the question if the 204 facing them would simply let shuttles land and extract the force. If push came to shove, 3/6 was among the force ordered to engage the Grubs to allow the shuttles to land and load the force.

"What do you think about those others?" BK asked on the P2P.

"I don't know, but it means something, that's for sure. Maybe they want to see what happens, just like us. I mean, this is the first time they've faced such a large force of us."

"They hit the Brotherhood and Confed battalions," she reminded him.

"Yeah, but there weren't that many of them there. Maybe 200 in all on the planet, and we've got that just here in our AO."

"It's gonna suck if the rest of their buddies decide to come and help out," she said.

Yeah, "suck" is an understatement.

"We'll see. We've got the shuttles ready to get us out of here if that happens."

"And we're the last ones to load out. It doesn't take a fucking genius to see how that'll turn out," she said, cutting the circuit.

Hondo chose not to think about that for now. If it came to that, so be it, but there was no use stressing out about something that might never happen. He took another sip of his ghost shit. It might give him the required nutrients to keep fighting ad infinitim, but it tasted like insipid cotton—not horrible, but hardly a treat for the taste buds. *When* they completed the mission (not "if") and were extracted, the Navy mess cooks would have a righteous meal laid out for them. That was good enough reason not to get killed on this dustball.

He flipped his display to the Order of Battle, which gave the positions of the Grubs, the human forces, and the Klethos. The humans and "their" Klethos had transponders that made their positions accurate. The Grubs were painted by the combat AIs as were the local Klethos. With the 204 remaining Grubs, that was pretty accurate—less so for the local Klethos. Task Force Pompeii had shifted in, closer to Task Force Rhine on the high ground. To Hondo's mild surprise, the Klethos screening force was still in place. They hadn't gone musth and charged the Grubs yet. The real test would be if they would abide by the plan when the time came. BK had bet him 100 credits they would break and go into musth-mode.

As he was watching his display, the first loose Grub rank, if you could call it that, eased into motion.

"We've got movement," the lieutenant passed. "This could be it."

Hondo zoomed in, and like a tsunami, the Grubs quickly reached 70 KPH as they barreled right down the valley at them.

"Get ready," Hondo needlessly passed to his team.

The local Klethos clashed with the front line, slowing down 20 or 30 of them. The humans would rather have had them out of the way so they could begin to employ their new long-range weaponry, but with the Klethos intermixed with the Grubs, that was not an option any longer.

Grubs fell, though. The local Klethos were dropping like flies, but five Grubs looked to be killed, five less that the

Marines would face. The rest of the Grubs bypassed the initial contact and flowed towards the waiting force. Task Force Dino, the name given to their Klethos, was arrayed 20 klicks in front of the Marines. This was going to be the tricky part of the plan.

The two forces clashed, and Hondo could almost imagine he could feel the ground shake. Other than a few modifications and an attempt to instill in mutual support to each other, the Klethos of Task Force Dino were not much different from the locals. They swarmed the Grubs like army ants on a caterpillar—only this caterpillar had its own bite. The surveillance drones, high above the battlefield, were left undisturbed, and they beamed images of the fight to the human fighters. A few Grubs were overwhelmed, although it was difficult to see if the Klethos' new training was having an impact. More Klethos fell to the power of the Grubs.

"Come on, any time now," BK passed.

Hondo watched as still more Klethos warriors fell. He kept expecting the order to come—the plan relied largely on it.

At last, the order was sent, and Hondo was probably not the only Marine to hold his breath waiting to see if the Klethos would obey it.

They did.

It was not a clean breaking contact. It came in is spurts, and some of the Klethos refused to disengage, but the bulk of them pulled to the flanks, allowing the Grubs to surge forward.

That was the second part of the plan—that the Grubs would allow for the break in contact and not pursue the Klethos.

"Now it's our turn," Sergeant Mbangwa passed. "Gear up, boys and girls."

The Marines were arrayed in a series of strongpoints, a defense in depth. The commander's intent was to slow and canalize the advancing Grubs. If the Grubs shifted to the planetary west and bypassed the Marines, not only would the town fall, but the entire operation would have been OBE. The Marines needed the Grubs to engage.

Three-Six was in the third rank, so-to-speak, of the defense. Three-Fourteen was ahead and slightly to their right, and One-Three was in the front rank and slightly to the left of Three-Six's position. The hope was that the seemingly weak spot between the battalions would canalize the Grubs into a winding advance, which would slow them down and open them up to more enfilade fire. It risked splitting up the Marine forces, but that was a risk the command had decided to take.

Hondo felt his pulse quicken as the Grubs rushed toward the Marines. They held steady, not veering to their right to bypass the defense.

At 12 klicks out, the first company of tanks opened up with their new guns—and had an immediate effect. Four of the slow-moving "Lightening" shells managed to penetrate the Grubs' shielding, and what were essentially mini-power stations came online for an instant, but that was long enough to fry the cellular circuitry of the enemy.

A cheer went up and down the lines. The tanks got off three volleys before the light spheres launched, and immediately the tanks stopped firing and powered up their shielding, which was related to Faraday cages. The cages took immense amounts of energy, which precluded them being used by PICS, but the Mannies had power to spare. Hondo held his breath as the spheres shot forward and released on the tanks. Alpha Company consisted of 17 battle tanks. When the light sphere hit them, seven were destroyed.

Shit!

The hope was that the shielding would protect the tanks, and they would wreak havoc on the Grubs. It did protect them, but not completely. In one moment, almost half of the tank company was gone.

The remaining tanks dropped their shields and fired two salvos before bringing them back up again. At the same time, the combat drones started firing. The drones were equipped with guns, energy weapons, and a missile whose warhead worked on the same principle as the tanks' Lightening shells. The air was filled with fire, and the Grubs answered back. Drones were dropping out of the sky, but not before another eight Grubs were killed.

Mobile artillery opened fire, the unmanned tubes on automatic. As more light spheres launched, the tubes joined in with the tanks in engaging their shielding. Light tendrils splashed against the tubes, knocking 75% offline after 30 seconds of sustained fire.

"Look at the numbers, BK. The Grubs are blowing through their energy," Hondo passed on the P2P.

He'd been watching the numbers on the energy feed, and the Grubs were expending energy at a furious rate. Some of the Grubs massed 25% less over the last ten minutes. Drones, tanks, and artillery tubes had been destroyed, but the shielding meant that the Grubs were expending more energy for each kill.

"That's one good thing," BK passed back. "Maybe they'll be the size of puppies by the time they reach us."

Not bloody likely, Hondo thought.

The disposition of the Marines was designed to disburse the Grubs, but that meant some relatively untouched Grubs would make it to the battalion's position. There wasn't going to be any rear echelon forces in the battle.

As the Grubs closed in, Marines opened up with their mid-range weapons: missiles, mortars, and heavy machine guns. None of these had the powerpacks to manage the shielding, so the missiles were offset to the Marines firing them. The hope was that when the Grubs took out the launchers, they wouldn't realize that the Marines 20 meters to the side were the ones who'd just fired them.

"Pompeii's on the move," Sergeant Mbangwa passed. "Now we hold them."

Hondo could see the Confederation-led force start to move into the high ground. So far, everything was going roughly according to plan—and that was worrying him. No plan ever survived contact with the enemy, so he was waiting for things to go to shit.

At three klicks, the energy cannons opened up. Hondo still didn't have a direct line of sight to one of the Grubs, but on the feeds, it looked as if the Grubs were bathed in coronas of blue light that fairly danced off their skins. The Grubs seemed to put the advance into a previously unobserved gear as they fairly leapt forward, seemingly intent to simply bowl over the front line of Marines.

One-Three—along with the other battalions arrayed across the 30-klick front—would have something to say about that. The Marines opened up with their entire array of weapons.

And the Klethos didn't like that at all.

Many of them swerved to the sides, light tendrils reaching out to engage individual Marines. A second wave of combat drones swept over the high ground on either side, peppering the Grubs with incendiaries as they engaged the Marines. The hope was to overload the Grubs, but they didn't seem to have their offensive power diminished. Hondo gave a quick look at the energy display. The Grubs were still in full attack mode, but they were burning up mass.

With the Marines fighting—and dying—twenty or thirty Grubs pushed through the gap between One-Three and Two-Seventeen, two of the three battalions on the front line. If they turned to flank either of the battalions, things were going to get dicey, but they kept advancing, right at Three-Six.

"Come on, Jaegers! Make your momma's proud," the battalion CO passed on the net

Not that memorable, but not bad, either, Hondo thought as he ran through his PICS stats one more time. With power still at 93% and a full combat load, he was as ready as he was ever going to be. He ran a quick check on his fire team. The other three Marines were combat-ready, too.

From above them, drones launched a salvo of both missiles and meson beams. Traces reached down from the sky to impact on the Grubs, but they kept advancing. Several troikas merged their light tendrils to shoot beams into the sky, knocking down drones. While no Grub was killed, they were expending energy, and the two Mannie platoons located within the Three-Six AOR opened fire. Hondo didn't know if it was because the Grubs had been depleted by the drones or if the Mannies were simply too powerful, but three Grubs exploded, their final reservoir of energy released all at once.

And then the rest of the Grubs hit the battalion's lines, and Hondo's world contracted down to three Grubs that merged their tendrils to take out one of the Mannies and then charged Kilo Company's position. The PICS Marines opened up with their mid-range weapons, needing the Grubs to close in before the new flamethrowers and the grappling hooks could be deployed.

One of the Grubs veered to the side and started rumbling right at First Squad.

"Ain't no thing, boys and girls. Just like back on the Purge," Sergeant Mbangwa passed, his voice devoid of stress.

Except there're no do-overs here, Hondo noted as the Grub closed the distance.

His readouts said the Grub was at 59%, but it looked huge to Hondo—huge and mighty pissed off. And it was heading right at Valúlfur. He couldn't let her take the brunt of the attack.

"Shift right," he ordered the fire team. "Now!"

Hondo side-hopped, something the PICS was not designed to do, but it got him into the path of the Grub. He powered up his shoulder launcher and and fired his RPR, the 20mm rocket plowing into its fleshy side. Hondo could see the Grub's skin heave around the spot as the warhead exploded.

The Grub raised its front up again, and Hondo could swear it was looking at him. He started to bolt to the right when a tendril of light hit him, this display almost blinded.

"Let's get more on him!" he passed before he realized his comms were fried. On his display, his shielding was dropping like a rock.

He caught a glimpse of a grappling hook as it flew over the beast, the line draping it.

"Come on, people! I need some help here!" he shouted, oblivious to the fact that no one could hear him.

His alarm went off, a beep-beep-beep telling him that he was redlining.

"I know, I know, he shouted, trying to dodge out of the way but the tendril followed him like a martin on a squirrel. He wasn't going to shake it.

The beep turned into a steady alarm. He had seconds left. He tried to dart to the left, but his PICS refused to move. It was dead, and unless something happened, so would he.

He still had his grappling hook. He knew he didn't have enough time, and the range was long, but he wasn't going to go out without a fight. He opened his visor shield and started cranking up his PICS arm. He got it aligned with the Grub up ahead and pulled back on the release. Nothing happened. The hook didn't launch. He tried again with the same result.

As much as it might seem to Hondo, though, the battle wasn't just between the Grub and him. His fellow Marines were attacking, and flames enveloped the Grub. It writhed and raised its front quarter, turning towards a charging Marine and unleashing a torrent of light tendrils that haloed the Marine in a bright corona.

Hondo didn't wait to see what happened to the Marine. He pulled the emergency molt, pulled up his legs, and slid out the back of his PICS. Hitting the ground hard, he then rolled to his feet, trying to orient himself. The air crackled with energy, his nose burning with ionization. A flash of heat hit him from the side.

Hell, second time in a row I lose my PICS. OK, Hondo. Time to step it up.

He didn't want to calculate the odds of losing his PICS two battles in a row, and more importantly, surviving the experience. Feeling naked in his long johns, he sidled to the front of his motionless PICS. The grappling hook was loaded and ready, and at first glance, he couldn't see why it hadn't fired. The why, though, wasn't important now. He needed to employ it.

The new grappling hook was a modular weapon with launcher and hook attached to the PICS' weapons jack. As with all weapon pods, it was designed to be quickly interchanged with another system. Hondo gave it a shake, and then he reached around to the base of the arm and grabbed the release lever. The armorers had a tool to flip the lever, a tool that Hondo didn't have.

No matter. Marine elbow grease would have to do the trick. He jammed his fingers under the tip of the lever and pulled. It might have budged, but that would have been hopeful thinking.

Something clanged off of the chest carapace of his PICS, making him duck. The battle was still raging around him. A hundred meters away, the Grub had at least a dozen light tendrils deployed.

Hondo jumped up on his PICS' extended arm. Squatting, he jammed the fingers of both hands under the lip of the lever, then with a huge grunt, pushed up with his legs. The lever gave, flipping open and smacking his left hand as Hondo fell over backward to the ground.

His hand was bruised and bloody, but he couldn't tend to it now. He scrambled back up to the arm, then lifted the grappling hook pod and dropped it to the ground. He jumped down, then bent to lift the module.

There was a reason that Marines fought in PICS—well many of them, but one being that they increased the strength of a Marine. The grappling hook pod was small as PICS weapons modules went, but it still massed a good hundred kilos. Hondo was by no means a weak Marine, but still, it was a heavy load. With a grunt, he lifted it to what Marines for some reason called the "John Wayne" position, catch assembly at his right hip, left hand outstretched and holding the handle over the stock.

Marines were all around him—some were fighting, some were motionless. At least one Marine was molting from a PICS, but Hondo didn't have time to help out. He had a target, a besieged Grub 100 meters ahead.

Part of the white skin had tinges of brown, like toasted coconut. Hondo felt a thrill course through him. Marines around him, probably his friends, had died, but it was obvious that the Grub was in a bad situation. It was visibly smaller, and its light tendrils seemed more haphazard. It shook its head back and forth, as if panic was setting in—if Grubs even felt panic.

A light tendril swept passing him, missing his feet by a meter, the air snapping with ionization. Hondo darted to the side, too late to have done anything. If he felt naked before, that feeling just quadrupled. He had no shielding, and 20 microns of polyamilyn long johns weren't going to do much. One touch, and he'd be KIA.

He pushed that thought out of his mind and forged forward. He didn't have sights on his grappling hook, so he'd have to rely on Kentucky windage to get it on target. The closer in he was, the better chance he'd have to hit the damned thing.

A Marine in a PICS rushed past him, almost knocking him aside as his flamethrower engulfed the Grub. If the enemy was in panic mode, that didn't seem to affect its ability to defend itself. Three tendrils struck the Marine, and as they converged, the bluish light turned a searing white. Tiny filaments of light bounced off the Marine toward him, and Hondo hit the deck, bouncing painfully off the grappling hook module. Ten meters away, the Marine's outgoing fire quit, and a moment later, his PICS seemed to slough apart, almost turning molten.

"You son-of-a-bitch!" he shouted, getting back to his feet.

He dodged around the dead Marine, his focus locked onto the Grub, which was now slowly backing up. "Slow" was relative. It was still faster than Hondo was on foot, lugging the grappling hook. It was pulling away from him.

He was now about 70 meters away, within range, but farther than he wanted to be. But the gods of war had dealt the cards, and Hondo was going to have to play them.

He came to a stop, took two deep breaths, and adjusted the muzzle of the launcher. The hook would fire in an arc, and he had to make sure that not only was he on target laterally, but he had to make sure he didn't over or undershoot.

Now or never, Hondo!

He pulled the trigger release . . . and nothing happened. He looked down to see what was wrong, but everything looked fine. Then it hit him. The release was designed for the PICS power, not Marine-power. He'd have to put some muscle into it.

He aimed again, and with a stronger effort, yanked on the release. With a clunk, the string shot forward, sending the grappling hook into the air. The effort he'd made, though, jerked the launcher just enough so that he thought he'd missed, but a blast of something hitting the Grub in its left side made it swerve right into the path of the hook. The metal tines sunk into its side, and the charge was released. Hondo could see flesh shudder, and for a moment, the light tendrils failed.

That was enough. Marines converged on it, firing every weapon they had. More grappling hooks reached out, and several hit almost simultaneously. A high-pitched wail made Hondo wince, and it took a moment for him to realize that it was the Grub making the noise, the first time he'd known they could make a sound. Light tendrils still emanated from it, but most seemed to be haphazard without a specific target.

"Shit, it's going to blow," Hondo said as he turned around to run.

He made it barely five meters before a bright white light hit him from behind, but without a punch. He turned back, and the Grub, or what was left of it, was collapsing in on itself. It may have tried to explode, but something had interfered, making it more of a fizzle.

Regardless, the thing was dead, and Hondo wanted to shout to the sky. They'd taken it out . . . no, that was too sanitary a phrase. They'd *killed* the mother fucker.

He wanted to celebrate, but the battle was not over. This was just one engagement. The battle was probably over for him, though, at least offensively. Without a weapon, he was simply a spectator.

He looked back at the half-melted PICS. Curiosity mixed with dread, he stepped over to see the name tag embossed on the carapace.

Part of it was melted away, but the last few letters were still visible: ". . .úlfur."

Oh, hell, Sunrise.

The feeling of warrior exuberance fled as he looked at the mass of junk that had been one of his Marines.

His Marines.

As a fire team leader, he only had three Marines in his mini-command, and now Sunrise Valúlfur was KIA. He was supposed to make sure she survived in one piece, that she got back home on Percy to her family, to her younger brother who wanted nothing more than to join her in the Corps.

He wondered if he was the only survivor, and that filled him with guilt.

"Nice shooting, Hondo!" someone shouted at him.

He wheeled around, and as if on cue, BK, also in her long johns, was waving at him from 30 meters away, her combat knife clasped in her hand. Relief swept through him. At least she had survived as well. He ran over to her, and she enveloped him in a hug, slapping his back.

"Way to go, Hondo. You nailed the sucker, and I think that was the turning point."

"Sunrise didn't make it. That's her," he said, pointing at the slagged PICS.

"Oh, shit. That's fucked up. What about Xeras?"

"I don't know. I'm kinda without comms, now."

"Yeah, me, too. I feel naked out here now," she said, making a sweep with her arms to indicate the light show surrounding them. "Second time me and you are in a fight in just our long johns. Is this becoming a habit?"

Hondo shrugged and said, "I sure hope not."

"So, what do we do now? I mean, we can't very well fight, right?"

"We stay out of the way unless we can figure out something. Maybe try and salvage another weapons module on one of the KIA?"

"Copacetic. Should we check . . . uh, you know?"

Hondo looked back to Sunrise. He doubted there was anything there they could salvage, and even if her flamethrower was still functional, which he doubted, he didn't think they could man-pack it. Still, it was worth a shot.

The two looked over the PICS. It had been breached, and the smell of cooked flesh hit them hard. Hondo had to fight to keep his gorge from rising.

"Why were we able to survive and molt when she . . . ?" he asked, not finishing the sentence.

"The gods of war, Hondo. You know that."

But he didn't "know that." Hondo thought there was something else involved, something they needed to figure out.

The two Marines jogged over to the next downed PICS. It looked relatively whole, but it hadn't molted. The Marine was still inside.

"Do we open it?" BK asked, voicing what Hondo had been asking himself.

If the Marine inside was hurt but alive, then it might be best to simply leave him or her inside the PICS for whatever protection it could offer. However if someone was hurt badly, he or she might need medical care.

"Let's crack it open and see," Hondo said after a moment's contemplation.

Every PICS had an interior and exterior molt lever. BK reached up high, opened the panel access, and pulled down on the red lever. Slowly, the back of the PICS began to crack open. Hondo leaned forward, afraid of what he'd see.

"Who's there?" a weak voice called out.

"Corporal McKeever, First Platoon, Kilo Company."

"Kilo? Three-Six? How the fuck did I get in with you guys? I'm Sergeant Derek Boister, Mike Three-Nine."

Hondo looked back at BK in surprise. If the sergeant was with Three-Nine, then either he or the two of them—three with Sunrise—were way out of position. BK shrugged.

"Uh . . . are you OK, Sergeant?" he asked.

"No, I'm not fucking OK. I'm out of action, and I don't know where the hell my squad is," he answered, both stress and pain evident in his voice.

"I mean, do you need medical help?"

"Yes, I need it. Wait . . . I mean, I will need it, but I think I'm stable."

"Do you want us to help you out, or do you want to stay inside until the battle's over?"

"Are we winning?" the sergeant asked.

"Uh, I'm not sure. I mean, we just killed one here, but the fighting is still all around us," Hondo said, looking around.

And 350 meters away, three Grubs appeared together, light tendrils hitting Marines.

"Oh, shit," BK said.

"We're leaving you inside, Sergeant. I think if you're out-of-action that they'll leave you alone."

"Wait, what's happening?"

"We've got company coming, three of them."

He looked to the front of the PICS and saw the grappling hook on the combat suit's right arm.

"Hey, Sergeant, is your hook cocked?"

"No, I got hit before I could cock it."

"Can you do it manually? I think we might need it?"

"Manually? Maybe, but I'm not sure I can maneuver the arm," he said, defeat in his voice. "Sorry, about that. I'm kind of hurting."

"If you can cock it, I can take the thing and man-pack it."

"What? How?"

"He already did it. Took out a fucking Grub, too," BK said. "But you need to get at it, Sergeant. They're coming now."

"No shit? Uh, OK. Let me try."

There was a pause, then Hondo could hear grunting from inside the PICS. He stepped over to the arm, and he could see the launcher string ease back ever-so-slowly.

The sound of coughing reached him, and the string stopped.

"Come, on, Sergeant, you're almost there."

The three Grubs were 200 meters to the north and engaging Marines who were swarming them.

The string started back again, and twenty seconds later, it slipped into the release slot.

"That's it," Hondo shouted as he released the pod and lowered it to the ground.

BK tried to help, but that wasn't working, so Hondo said, "I've got it," getting back in John Wayne mode.

"We'll be back for you," he shouted to the sergeant as he and BK started forward to join the fight.

"Wish I had a sling," he said as they half-jogged, half-walked.

"You're doing fine, Hondo. You're the man."

"You aren't armed, BK. Hold back."

"There ain't no safe place here, Hondo. I'm sticking with you," she said, brandishing her knife as if she was about to stick a Grub.

He was about to order her to hold back, but she was right. There wasn't a safe place on the battlefield. At least this way, they knew where each other was.

At least 30 or even 40 Marines had swarmed the last Grub. Hondo didn't have time to count, but it seemed as if fewer were in the fight to face the three in front of them. It didn't look good.

Coming in from the Grub's left flank, Hondo and BK were alone as they advanced. The Grubs ignored the two, which was good as a single touch of a light tendril would take care of them both. They had to cross some broken ground, and with Hondo lugging the module, it took them almost three minutes to cross 150 meters to get close to them.

"This is good enough. Be ready to run," he told BK.

He knelt, aimed the best he could, and with a short prayer, jerked the trigger release. With a snap, the hook launched . . . and sailed right over his target . . . and hit the Grub behind it.

"Good shot," BK shouted as the hook released its charge and the Grub raised up its front quarter and swung back and forth.

Hondo didn't bother to correct her. He watched, hoping to see something more dramatic, but while the Grub was obviously bothered, it wasn't out of action. It was still in the fight, dishing it out.

"Shit," he said quietly.

"You hurt it," BK told him.

"Not enough. Look at them. I see what, maybe ten Marines against three Grubs?" he said, not bothering to hide the bitterness in his voice.

One of the Grubs, his intended target, started convulsing, slinging light tendrils wildly. The three Grubs converged their tendrils, and the white beam shot up into the sky, knocking out the drone—or ship, Hondo didn't want to contemplate—that had hit them.

A moment later, the three focused back on the Marines facing them, the closest Grub decidedly damaged but still alive.

"That's about it here, then," Hondo said.

He wished there was something the two of them could do, but this wasn't a Hollybolly fantasy adventure flick. This was real life.

Two more Marines went down and he and BK watched, bitter bile rising in their throats. It seemed obscene that they were standing there, so close to the violence but little more than spectators.

Hondo was about to turn away, unable to watch anymore when the Grubs suddenly turned together away from the two Marines. Intense fire reached out to envelope the three Grubs. Within moments, the wounded Grub exploded.

"It's about fucking time," BK said. "The cavalry's here."

Hondo clambered up on a large rock to see. Four or five hundred meters away, he could see Klethos warriors rushing into the battle, an unstoppable tide of angry warriors.

He turned to look to the east. If everything was going according to plan, Task Force Pompeii was closing the pincher. He couldn't see anything in that direction, but at least the Klethos had stuck to the operations order.

Now the question was if the Marines had been able to attrite the Grubs enough for the enveloping forces to close the deal. The Marines had paid a heavy price in blood with no assurances that it would be enough.

A low rumble reached him, the sound of Klethos voices as they rushed the Grubs.

Something almost pulled him off the rock, and he swung around ready to strike back, but it was BK, grabbing him by the waist so she could see. There wasn't much room where they could stand, but with her leaning against him, they both had a grandstand view of this tiny part of the battle.

The Klethos were fearless—and crazy, but there was a method to the madness. These weren't the Klethos of old, rushing into the melee. Hondo could see teamwork, something he hadn't really observed back on Purgamentium when they were training together. Whoever had been working with them after the split had done wonders, he thought.

The two remaining grubs edged their hind ends together, spreading their heads out into a V as they engaged the Klethos. And they were effective. Klethos after Klethos fell, but more stepped into the fallen's places.

At 100 meters away, the Klethos shifted to their grappling hooks, and wave after wave of the hooks reached out, slamming into the Grubs. At that point, Hondo knew the fight was over, even if the Grubs didn't. They increased their output, light tendrils sweeping the Klethos, but without the duration needed to tally kills. This was the end game, and Hondo could feel the kill intensity of the Klethos as they closed in for the kills.

With a blinding flash of light, the two Grubs exploded, the pressure wave knocking the two Marines off the rock. Both jumped up, unhurt, and screaming out in unabashed exultation. They jumped back up on the rock, and there was nothing left of the Grubs. More Klethos were down, probably taken out by the Grub's death knell explosions, but the fight was over—decidedly over.

Over here, but not in the entire AOR. The flashing lights and sounds of fighting were evidence enough that while this fight was done, the battle was not. Still, in his fire team's small piece of ground in the AOR, Hondo had seen four Grubs killed. If this was by any means representational, then the human-Klethos task force had a chance of actually winning a battle. There were thousands more Grubs on the planet, but a victory here would be only the first as humanity mobilized. A victory here might convince the Brotherhood and the rest to rejoin the effort.

The surviving Klethos were not done fighting. They rushed past the two Marines, not sparing them a glance as they looked for another fight.

"I can't believe it," BK said. "I really didn't think we could pull it off."

"We haven't pulled off anything yet," Hondo reminded her. "The battle isn't over."

"Yes, it is, Hondo. The Grubs might not know it, but it's over. We've beat them."

Hondo wasn't so sure about that. He was hopeful, but he wasn't about to declare victory.

"Let's go get that sergeant," he said, refusing to give rise to false hope.

The two walked over to where Sergeant Boister was still in his PICS. The sergeant was noticeably weaker. Hondo had a suspicion that he was hurt more than he let on.

"We're going to get you out of there," Hondo said.

Molting out of a PICS took a little Cirque de Soleil maneuvering, and it quickly became clear that the sergeant wasn't up to it.

"We're going to have to get him," he told BK as he started to climb up on the motionless PICS' back.

BK pulled him back and said, "This is mine. I'm half your size."

Hondo started to argue that he was stronger than her, but as she scrambled up the PICS, he bit that back. She had a point—she was smaller and could worm her way inside easier than he could. More than that, he realized she needed this. She'd been merely an observer while he lugged the heavy grappling hook pod into the last fight.

Her top half disappeared into the back of the PICS, and in a moment, her legs and butt were wiggling as she struggled with the sergeant. She started to slide back out when the sergeant let out a yell of agony. Hondo climbed up the side of the PICS, ready to help her. With a final heave, she pulled the sergeant into view, and Hondo helped get him out, then gently laid him on the ground.

And he didn't know what to do with him.

All Marines had basic first aid, but there wasn't a mark on the sergeant. What was wrong with him was on his inside, and Hondo didn't have a clue what to do. He wasn't sure any of the corpsmen would, either. He heeded a doctor's care. The sergeant's hands were curled within themselves, and Hondo vaguely remembered that meant something, only he didn't remember what.

"Just relax, Sergeant. Someone's going to be here, soon," he said.

"Did we win?" the sergeant asked, barely coherent.

Hondo shot a glance at BK, who was mouthing "yes."

"Sure did, Sergeant. We've won. We're just waiting on Doc to get here to get you fixed up."

"Fucking A skippy. Of course, we won. We're fucking Marines," he muttered before slipping into unconsciousness.

The sounds of fighting began to die down. An hour later, the AOR was silent. BK took that for granted. She knew they'd carried the day. Hondo hoped they had.

Thirty minutes later, as the two watched over the sergeant, two PICS Marines came striding into view. They spotted the two Marines and veered to meet them. Hondo felt a surge of relief. He'd been imagining all sorts of bad scenarios, all centered on the three of them being alone on the planet.

They stood up as the two PICS Marines approached them.

"That you, Corporal Mckeever?" a familiar voice reached them over one of the PICS exterior speakers.

"PFC Xeras?"

"One and the same. We thought you two had bought it. We came back to try and recover your bodies, so, you know . . ."

"Sunrise is KIA," Hondo said.

"Are you sure?" BK asked, her voice catching.

Hondo realized he hadn't told her, and he said, "Very sure."

"Shit," she said quietly.

"Hey, I've got to keep going," the other Marine spoke for the first time. "We've only got an hour."

"OK, see you back at the AA," PFC Xeras said.

"An hour?" Hondo asked.

"Well, we've been given an hour to try and recover the KIA . . . uh, and the WIA, and then get back to the Assembly Areas so we can load out. Can you make it? And who is that?" she asked, pointing with her gauntlet.

"That's a sergeant from Three-Nine. He's in rough shape," BK answered.

"OK, I'll call in for a medevac."

"Wait a minute. You said, 'Load out.' Where're we going now? The main city?"

"Right now? We're going to the ships and sit in orbit for a while, then back to Purgamentium, Corporal. We've won."

"This battle, yes. But there are a lot more Grubs here."

"Not for long. I guess you hadn't heard. We really won. The Grubs are taking off, in droves. We're going to sit in orbit until the last one leaves, then send in recovery teams for the rest of our KIA, but it looks like we kicked their asses. They're running away."

"Running away?" Hondo said. "Just like that?"

"Just like that. I mean, the CG, he doesn't completely trust them, so that's why we're hanging around to make sure, but we killed us every one of them here. Us and the local Klucks."

"I knew it," BK said. "We're fucking Marines, and no one can stand against us."

Marines, Confeds, Rangers, Legionnaires, and a host of others. Not to mention the Klucks. But yeah, I guess we did win, he thought. *Holy shit, we did it!*

PURGAMENTIUM

Chapter 31
Skylar

"That's it. The last Dictymorph has left the planet and is in full flight mode," Christoff Hans shouted out.

Sky joined the rest in cheers. Someone hugged her, and she didn't care. She jumped up and down in excitement, excitement that had been building once it was clear that the battle had turned into their favor.

"We did it!" L'Teesha shouted as she ran up to Sky and pounded on her shoulders.

"You did it, L'Teesha. Those disruption hooks were your idea. You won the battle," Sky insisted.

Knight Hastert grabbed L'Teesha by the shoulder and spun her around, giving her a huge kiss.

More than a few of the scientists were half-sloshed. Sky had held off drinking until the last Dictymorph had left, and now she was ready. Gentle Bosovitch was walking by, a can of Mountain Amber Ale in his hand. Sky snagged it and took a deep swallow before holding it back out.

"Keep it," Gentle said. There's more where it came from.

Sky was still trying to comprehend what had just happened. The Marines, the "fixing force," as some called them, the "bait" as others called them, had fought hard, but they were losing the battle. Then, just like in the animations shown to them in the brief, the rest of the human forces and the wonderful Klethos and converged on the enemy, crushing them in a pincher movement. One side of the pincher had done a lot more damage. The Confederation force, Task Force Pompeii, had barely reached the battlefield and engaged the Dictymorphs by the time the Klethos had swept through, saving the remaining Marines and killing the last of the enemy.

Sky had been serious in what she said to L'Teesha. The disruption hooks had been proven effective in the hands of the Marines, but they'd been deadly in the hands of the Klethos. Their allies had attacked as if possessed, and as Sky had watched the feeds, she was suddenly very glad they were on the same side. Some of her colleagues had begun to dismiss the Klethos given their lack of human tactical theory, but the fight had been a reminder as to why the first Klethos-human engagements a century before had been decidedly lopsided, and not in the humans' favor.

Then, the miracle occurred. Not only were the 200-plus Dictymorphs in the battle defeated, but even before the last one fell, Dictymorphs from around the planet began to engage their space-going capability. Like the dead rising on Judgment Day, they simply began to rise off the planet's surface, reaching space and accelerating out of the system.

Ale still in her hand, she accepted a hug from someone she didn't recognize.

"Dicty, Dicty, run so fast . . . Dicty, Dicty we kicked your ass!" someone shouted in a chant before repeating it. Within moments, others joined in, jumping up and down and yelling the "kicked your ass" part at the top of their lungs. A conga line formed, thirty strong, chanting the little made-up ditty over and over again as it wended its way through the revelry.

Sky was about to join when she saw Bill Boswell standing to the side, his face frozen in a frown.

"Hey, there, sourpuss. Get happy. Like they're saying," she said as she reached the Marine, "we kicked their asses."

He shrugged, then took her ale and drained it. The smile she expected failed to make an appearance.

"What's a matter with you? This is our first victory, the first of many."

"We kicked their asses, Sky? Really?"

"Yeah, really. There aren't any more of them on the planet. We did it. L'Teesha over there," she said, pointing at her fellow scientist, number four in the conga line, "her hooks did it, I think."

"Grappling hooks deployed by Marines, soldiers, and Klucks, Sky."

"Well, yeah. But we developed it," she said, sweeping her arm around to encompass all the scientists and engineers.

"And how many of us died?" he asked bitterly.

"Well, none, of course," Sky said, confused by his reaction.

"We've got well north of 7,000 Marine KIA and another 3,000 from the rest of the human forces. The Klucks probably lost 2,000. All to take out 206 Grubs."

"But not just that, Bill. The rest of the Dictymorphs, they left the planet."

"A strategic victory, to be sure. Even a tactical one, if you don't' consider the butcher's bill. A proof of concept, sure. But 'we,'" he said, repeating her arm sweep, "didn't kick anyone's ass. We might have provided the tools, but we weren't in danger. We didn't risk our lives. We didn't make the ultimate sacrifice.

"Sorry, Sky, but I just can't celebrate the loss of 12,000 lives."

He crushed the can of ale, then dropped it on the floor.

"You celebrate, if you want. I'm out of here."

Sky stared after him, her mouth dropped open.

But this is a victory, right. I mean, we won, right.

She turned to look back at the celebrating crowd, and suddenly she wasn't in the mood to join them. Bill was right. So many dead were not a cause for celebration.

Instead of joy, she now felt shame. More than that, though, she felt a compulsion to get back to work. Her job was to help find the vulnerabilities of the Dictymorphs so next time—and there would be a next time—so many young men and women wouldn't have to die.

Chapter 32
Hondo

"Corporal Hondo McKeever, reporting as ordered, sir!"

"Stand at ease, Corporal," Lieutenant Colonel Rainer said. "First time we've talked since the battle, right son?"

Uh . . . sir, we've never talked

"Yes, sir. First time since the fight."

"I've been busy, you know. Lots of messages home," he said, his voice fading a bit as his eyes drifted down to stare at his desktop.

Shit, you've got all those death messages back to the families, Hondo thought, feeling guilty for his flippant thought of a moment ago. He stood at a parade rest, not saying anything.

The battalion CO shook his head, looked back at to him, and then said, "I've discussed your performance during the battle with Lieutenant Copek and Staff Sergeant Aster."

He nodded over Hondo's shoulder where the company XO—commander, now, with Captain Montgomery killed in the fight—stood with the staff sergeant. Lieutenant Silas had also been KIA, and the staff sergeant was the acting platoon commander until a lieutenant came aboard to take over.

"I've also gone over the recordings. Pretty ballsy, there, Corporal, taking on a Grub in just your long johns."

Hondo didn't know how to respond to that, so he took the safest course of action and remained silent.

"I also discussed your action with Lieutenant Colonel Suarez," he continued.

Hondo didn't have a clue as to who this Suarez was, but he didn't bother to ask.

"I happen to agree with her assessment. After you hit the Grub with your hook, its reading went haywire, and it started expending energy like crazy. You may not have killed the thing, but you fucked it up but good. And that allowed the rest of your fellow Marines to finish it off. All of this, I don't have to add, basically naked. One touch of a light tendril and you would have been KIA."

Hondo didn't know what surprised him more, the fact that the colonel evidently thought he'd done something noteworthy leading to the kill, or that a senior officer used the word "fucked."

"What you did, son, that was pretty amazing, not that I'd expect anything less from a Jaeger. You did the battalion proud."

"Thank you, sir, but I didn't do anything anyone else wouldn't have done."

"Maybe so, son, but the fact remains that you did it, not anyone else. Now, I'm not here to blow sunshine daffodils up your ass. Frankly, you did what I would have expected, and from what Staff Sergeant Aster tells me, what he or Lieutenant Silas would have expected. Still, expected or not, your actions were noteworthy, and I called you in here to tell you you're being recommended for the Navy Cross."

Hondo felt as if he'd been kicked in the stomach by a mule.

A Navy Cross?

"You can close your mouth, son. Don't want the bugs to fly in now, right?" the CO said coming around the desk to shake his hand.

Hondo snapped his mouth shut, taking the colonel's hand.

A Navy Cross?

He didn't know what to say.

"Now, it has to be approved by the First Ministry, but all our awards are being fast-tracked, so we should know soon. Congratulations, son. I'm proud of you.

"Now, go stand beside Staff Sergeant Aster for a moment. I want you here for this.

"Sergeant Mbangwa, please call in PFC Xeras."

The staff sergeant shook Hondo's hand as he took his place beside him. He stood at attention as a nervous-looking Xeras stepped inside and reported to the CO. Hondo was still in shock and barely listened as the colonel greeted Xeras. It wasn't until he heard the colonel say "instrumental in the deaths of two Grubs" that he was jerked back into the here and now.

What's this about two Grubs?

Hondo had debriefed Xeras and BK, and he knew the PFC had been in the thick of the fighting, being part of two attacks on Grubs, but "instrumental?" What had he missed? She hadn't said she'd done anything extraordinary.

". . . one of only 13 flamethrower Marines to survive the fight, you know."

"Yes, sir, I heard that."

"The Grubs were targeting all of you, and for a reason. You were killing them. But, I've got to ask you, the first one, you had a stand-off range of 100 meters. Why did you charge it so close?"

"Well, sir, I saw that it took our Corporal McKeever, and that pissed me off royally. He's my team leader, and that piece of white puke wasn't going to get away with that. So, I don't know. I just kinda lost it, sir, and I got in tight and flamed it but good."

"Well, that you did, PFC. And the second?"

"I kinda got separated from my unit, sir, and I thought everyone in my squad was dead. So, when the Klucks . . . I mean Klethos, sir, no disrespect, when they came running in all crazy like, I just followed them. They swarmed a Grub, and when it was all distracted, I just ran up and fired its asshole. I mean, I think it was its asshole. I mean, sir, I was pissed, and I had to do something."

"Remind me not to get you pissed at me, Marine."

"Oh, never sir!" she said, her voice in a panic.

The colonel laughed, then said, "I'm not worried, about that. And that's not why I had the sergeant major call you in. Your actions have drawn notice, significant notice. The UAM has released a recording of what you did, and the public reaction is significant."

"Really, sir? They can see it back on Emerson?"

"Yes, of course on Emerson."

"Wicked copacetic," she said more to herself.

"There's something else, though. The UAM command has recommended you for a Gold Starburst."

That floored Hondo. The Gold Starburst was the UAM equivalent to the Federation Nova. Marines were rarely in a position to earn a UAM medal for valor, but even so, it was rare for a Marine, especially an enlisted Marine, to be awarded one.

"What's a Gold Starburst, sir?"

"What's that? 'That' is a pretty amazing accomplishment for a Marine. You can ask Lieutenant Copek after you're dismissed, and he can bring you up to speed."

Hondo thought the colonel was more amused than anything else that Xeras had no idea what the award signified."

"Nothing is assured, and with the UAM, the military command is rarely in synch with the civilian leadership. You being Federation could impact that as well."

"I'm sorry, sir, I'm confused."

The colonel laughed and said, "Don't worry about it, Lance Corporal. Whatever happens, happens."

"Uh . . . begging the colonel's pardon, sir, but I'm a PFC, not a lance corporal."

"Are you calling me a liar? Your commanding officer?" he asked with faux bluster.

Hondo thought Xeras was going to piss in her panties. She'd faced down not one, but two Grubs, and now she was terrified. She started to stammer out an apology when the CO held out a hand to stop her.

"I have the authority to offer field promotions up to corporal, and I think you rate one of those promotions. As of today, you are now a lance corporal. I've got the crossed rifles here, if you want to get it done now. Or you can get it done in front of the battalion during formation on Friday. Your choice."

"The whole battalion, sir?" she asked in barely a squeak.

Hondo almost laughed. Once again, she faced down two Grubs because she was "pissed," and now she was afraid of getting up before the battalion?

"Uh, now would be good sir. If the sir doesn't mind, sir."

"Now it is, then. Sergeant Major, if you would read the warrant?" he said as he took his place in front of her.

"Attention to orders!"

To all who shall see these presents, greeting:

Know Ye, that reposing special trust and confidence in the fidelity and abilities of Fiona L. Xeras, I do appoint her a Lance Corporal in the United Federation Marine Corps to rank as such from the twelfth day of April, in the year four hundred and thirty-three.

This appointee will therefore carefully and diligently discharge the duties of the grade to which appointed by doing and performing all manner of things thereunto pertaining. And I do strictly charge and require all personnel of lesser grade to render obedience to appropriate orders. And this appointee is to observe and follow such orders and directions as may be given from time to time by superiors acting according to the rules and articles governing the discipline of the military forces of the United Federation of States.

Given under my hand at United Assembly of Man Task Force Headquarter, Purgamentium, on this twelfth day of April, four hundred and thirty-three.

Tan Ranier
Lieutenant Colonel
Commanding

The colonel took off both of Xeras' PFC chevrons, then pinned the lance corporal insignia on her right collar.

"Congratulations, Lance Corporal. And should I ask Staff Sergeant Aster to put on the other?"

"Begging the sir's pardon, but could I have Corporal McKeever pin it on? If that's OK?"

"Of course, it's OK. It's your choice, and Corporal McKeever is an excellent one.

"Corporal?" he asked, holding out the other chevron.

Hondo was surprised. He'd ridden Xeras hard, and as the next junior Marine in the CO's office, he hadn't expected her to want him to do the honors. He marched forward, executed two left turns, and stopped in front of her. Taking the chevron from the colonel, he slowly and deliberately pinned it on her collar.

"Congratulations, Lance Corporal Xeras. I'm proud of you."

And he was. Even with her nomination for the Gold Starburst, even with his own nomination for the Navy Cross, simply being asked to pin on her new insignia filled him with pride and a sense of honor. Medals were one thing, awarded for actions past. No matter how rare that was, and no matter how many times Marines were promoted, the two didn't compare. Xeras had a choice in this, and that fact that she chose him humbled him.

For the first time since being promoted to corporal, he began to have an inkling of what it meant to be a leader of Marines.

Chapter 33
Skylar

"I still think they just bugged out," Hastert said.

"'Grubbed' out, you mean," Aurora added.

After three days of getting nowhere, Sky didn't have the energy to laugh. The working group had been tasked with determining why the thousands of Dictymorphs on K-3363 had "Grubbed out" en masse. The human-Kethos force had defeated the local Dictymorph force, but it had taken too many casualties. It could not have survived an all-out attack by even a portion of the rest of them. The task force command had contingency plans in place to extract the force if—and when, most people assumed—the Dictymorphs turned their attention to them, but even before the last one fell in the battle, the rest of them had started to leave the planet.

The burning question was why.

On the more optimistic side, suggested by L'Teesha, the Dictymorphs had their nose bloodied, possibly for the first time, and had left the Klethos corner of the galaxy for easier pickings. On the more pessimistic side, also suggested by L'Teehsa, was that they left as a feint and were now marshaling forces for an all-out attack throughout Klethos space.

Sky was torn between the two extremes, but the scientist in her had to acknowledge that was only a gut feeling based on no hard evidence. She was not above working from conjecture—her dissertation, after all, was largely based on conjecture, her take on the available data. This time, with the Dictymorphs, she had nothing, and she was hesitant to forward up an official opinion, an opinion that would probably help map out the human-Klethos way forward.

"Might I remind you that all we know is that they did leave the planet—"

"Unless they're staging just out of our scanner range waiting to return," Lars interrupted her.

"Like I said," Sky continued, "all we know is that they left the planet's surface. We don't know why. Yes, they could be sitting somewhere ready to pounce back onto the planet now that we've left, but we don't know that. And that's why we've been here for three days, to try and come to a consensus as to the why, not the what."

"Come on, Sky. You don't need to lecture us. We know why we're here," Gentle said.

Yes, I do need to "lecture" you; otherwise, nothing is going to get done.

"I'm not lecturing anyone. I'm just thinking aloud, trying to make sense of this. From what I've jotted down here, we've got no less than 14 potential explanations. It would help me get my head around all of this is we can narrow this down to maybe the three most likely reasons. Then, we can focus on those and see what we come up with. Gentle, what do you think are the most likely reasons?"

This is so transparent, she thought to herself. *Professing ignorance to move this along. They're going to see right through me.*

But they didn't.

Gentle sighed, then said, "Yes, it can be confusing, so let me simplify the basic points of the four or five I think are most likely. First, Knight could be basically correct. The Dictymorphs..."

I wanted just three, but I can deal with five, she thought as she gazed with what she hoped looked like rapt attention to her fellow xenobiologist.

Chapter 34
Hondo

"Happy Patron's Day," Sergeant Mbangwa said to the table, shaking everyone's hand.

"You, too, Sergeant. Jaegers rule!" Hondo said.

"Yep, Jaegers rule. Next Patron's Day celebration will be back on Alexander," he said.

A chorus of ooh-rahs broke out from the rest of the Marines.

"And hey, Soldier, I wanted to tell you I'm sorry about your Navy Cross. The first sergeant told me this afternoon."

"Ain't no thing, Sergeant. I'm not a Marine for some medal to put on my chest. I'm here for my fellow Marines," he said, sweeping an arm to indicate the rest of his tablemates.

"Fucking-A right," BK said.

What he said wasn't really true. Not the part about being there for his fellow Marines, but that it wasn't "no thing." He hadn't expected to be put in for the award in the first place, but once the CO had told him, the idea grew on him. Then today, only an hour before the celebration had begun, he'd been told his Navy Cross had been downgraded to a Silver Star. Which was still no shabby award, but he'd already begun to accept the idea of a Navy Cross. And to be honest, he was a bit pissed about the entire thing.

Not that he'd admit that to anyone else. Marines just didn't do that. He'd once read a quote from the old Earth general, Napoleon, about men doing anything for a bit of colored ribbon to put on their chest. It might be true in today's Corps as well, probably was true, in fact, but no one could admit it.

"Still, I think it sucks hind tit. But I'm just a mere sergeant, so what the hell do I know."

Sergeant Mbangwa moved on to the next table. Hondo was grateful for his words, though. It didn't cost the squad leader anything to say them, but they had an effect. That was the "leader" in squad leader being exhibited. He filed that away in his personal "how to be a leader of Marines" corner of his brain housing group.

"Do we have an exact date yet?" Fiona asked.

"No exact date, but I'm guessing about the 17th. Most of IV MEF is here already. We're up to swap out our PICS tomorrow morning, and then with about a three-week turnover, I'd say we start the redeployment about then," Paul Yetter said.

"We're first out, us and Two-Fourteen," Dixie added.

Hondo caught the look BK gave her friend, Gabriella Stanton, a lance corporal from First Tanks, who she'd invited to the battalion's Patron Day celebration. First Tanks was not redeploying yet, so the budding romance between the two was about to be cut off. BK had told Hondo it didn't matter, that she was just "having fun," but Hondo didn't believe that for one moment. His friend was smitten, pure and simple.

But that was life in the Corps. Relationships were difficult to maintain, especially for junior Marines. Even if married, a Marine had to be a sergeant before he or she would rate the extra pay and base housing.

BK might be disappointed, but Hondo was going to be happy to get off this rock and back to civilization. Alexander might not be his home planet, but it sure beat Purgamentium.

"The first thing I'm going to get is a big deluxe pizza a Fritos," Fiona said.

"Hell, Xeras, did you even get a chance to have one before you got shipped out here as RepMar?" Dixie asked.

"Eat me. Sure, I did. How else would I know about Fritos?"

"'Cause about every one of us old salts talk about it. So, between reporting in from boot to leaving for the Purge as a RepMar, how long did you have on Alexander?"

"Two weeks, but that was enough time to go to Fritos. Twice!"

The rest of the table erupted into laughter.

"Hell, I went twice a week for a year before we deployed here," BK said.

Hondo leaned back in his seat, listening to the banter. These were his friends, his family, and he'd never forget them. Some had been there since they first landed. Paul, BK, Dixie, Jorge. Sergeant Mbangwa. Others had joined them as RepMars, Replacement Marines, but they still made their impact like Fiona and Luke.

And there were those who'd they'd lost: Sam. Rosy. Doc Pataki. Sunrise. Tinman. Lieutenant Silas. They were still part of the platoon, part of him.

Hondo was just as anxious to get back as the rest of them, but he also felt the pang of the loss he knew he'd feel. They'd all get new orders once they were back. Dixie was not reenlisting. The rest of them would be scattered to the winds. Right now, celebrating the battalion's Patron's Day, might be the last time they'd ever be so close, and that made Hondo sad. Grateful that he had them in his life, but sad that this was all about to end. He almost wished that they weren't redeploying.

Almost.

"I love you guys," he said before realizing it.

"Love you, too, big guy," BK said. "Even if you can be a dickwad NCO."

"Back at you," Dixie said.

"Jaegers forever," Fiona added.

Paul just nodded and lifted his champagne glass to him in a silent toast.

The war with the Grubs wasn't going to be over anytime soon, and chances were that all of them would be back in the fight soon enough. With the Brotherhood and the rest gone, that left the Confed and the Federation to pick up most of the slack, and that meant a quarter of the Corps was now committed. Paul thought that might jump up to half before long, and Hondo tended to agree with that.

Hell, enough with the Grubs and the war. Just enjoy the evening, he told himself.

"Any more of that champagne?" he asked.

"They gave us one bottle for the entire table, and you think there's any left? What, are you high?" Paul asked.

"He ain't high on just one bottle," BK said. "But, if you NCOs won't be gung-ho pricks, I might have something back in the hootch."

"Might? And just where would you have scored something?" Paul asked.

"I'll never reveal my sources," she said, nudging Gabriella, who unsuccessfully failed to suppress her cat-eating grin.

"Oh, so a tanker's good for something?" Dixie asked.

"She's good for plenty of things," BK said to the catcalls of the others.

Gabriella had the courtesy of blushing.

Hondo looked around the hangar where the tables had been set up. At the head table, the CO and the senior guests were still seated, but the general had the look of somebody about to leave. As soon as they left, the rest of the battalion would be free to leave as well.

"Well, this NCO isn't a gung-ho prick, so I'm up for whatever you've got hidden away. As soon as the head table gets up, let's go sample it," Hondo said. "And I'm guessing that'll be in less than five minutes."

Paul looked over at the table and said, "I'm going with the over. You up for a tenner?"

"You're on. Ten it is. On my mark, now!"

Marines had a habit of betting on almost anything, and BK and Dixie made a side bet, Dixie going along with Hondo and BK with Paul. At two minutes, the head table still hadn't made any sign of leaving.

"You getting nervous?" Paul asked.

"Hell, no," Hondo lied. "You want to double it?"

"To twenty? That one glass of champagne's gone to your head."

"So, you're afraid?"

"Hell, no. You're on. We'll see soon enough, in about two minutes and forty more seconds."

They never reached the five minutes. With more than a minute left, a raucous siren filled the air outside the hangar. All talk ceased as Marines looked about in confusion. The siren was a warning, but of what?

A lieutenant with the gold braid of an aide rushed over from the portable comms suite that had been set up in the corner of the hangar. He bent over the general who listened for a moment, then jumped to his feet. He said something to the CO, then rushed out, the lieutenant and five other Marines in his wake.

The CO grabbed for the mic and said, "All hands, report to the armory immediately. Company commanders, to me now."

There was a stunned silence, and the CO added, "This is not a drill. We are under attack!"

Chapter 35
Skylar

Sky stared at Diane, the nominal head of the d'solle quad. If what she'd just said, almost in an off-handed manner, were true, then the humans were going to have to drastically rethink their strategy.

"Can you be more specific?" Creighton asked, his voice cracking.

As the head of the Klethos division, he should have known this rather pertinent fact, and he had to realize that this didn't reflect well on him or his team. Sky didn't care about his reputation, however. She did care about what Diane had just said.

"We are who we are, no more or no less. We are the Klethos," Diane responded.

"But you said that the Klethos here form a large percentage of your force."

"This is true."

"But that's a little more than 12,000 fighters," Colonel Hsih said, the senior military rep at the meeting.

Diane slowly blinked, which was the Klethos equivalent of a nod.

"That's impossible. How could you have . . . uh, *eliminated* 17 other species with so few warriors."

"It is the heart of the warrior, the honor, that succeeds in battle. Until we discovered you, no other race understood this. They were as the food animals we slaughter to eat."

Sky did some quick calculations in her head. From gleaning information given in dribs and drabs, they knew that there was only one warrior for every 500-1,000 Klethos. Assuming the 1,000-to-one ratio, and assuming that the battalions here on Purgamentium were 25% of the total force, then that meant that there were only 48,000,000 Klethos in existence. Humans numbered close to 200 billion.

"No wonder they wanted gladiatorial combat," Bill whispered beside her.

Sky was gobsmacked. The Klethos were better fighters when compared to humans, and they had the ability to nullify most human weapons. But no matter their fighting prowess or technology, there was no way 48,000 Klethos warriors could withstand 30 billion soldiers that humans could put in uniform if it came to that.

For the first time, Sky had to wonder if the Klethos had been playing the long con over the last century, leading humans to contribute their teeming masses to the fight against the Grubs.

The meeting with d'solle had been called to ask the Klethos to send more fighters to be trained in integrated tactics. They had asked for 50,000, and Diane had countered with 4,000, telling that that was all they could spare without leaving undefended the planets they thought the Dictymorphs would hit next.

The numbers just didn't make sense to Sky, and she was about to ask Diane about Klethos reproduction rates when a siren started blaring outside the building. Everyone looked at each other in confusion.

Beside her, Bill pulled out his PA. He looked at it for a moment before he jumped to his feet, a split second after Colonel Hsih.

The senior colonel shouted out, "We're under attack. All of you, stay inside the room. I'll send someone back for security. Bill, let's go."

"Don't move," Bill said to her before he dashed out of the conference room.

There was dead silence for a moment before everyone broke out talking at once.

"Who's attacking us? The Brotherhood?" Aurora asked.

The Brotherhood had taken an increasingly antagonistic stance toward the war effort, but Sky didn't think things had sunk to violence yet.

"It is the *ksree*," Diane announced, using the half-whistle Klethos name for the Dictymorphs.

"That's impossible," EC Stanislaw protested. "They're hundreds of light years away."

"The impossible is the fact," Diane said as the quad rose in unison.

They started for the door when Stanislaw said, "Wait. The colonel said to stay here!"

The muffled sounds of a gun of some sort reached them.

"The *kshree* are here. We will join our warriors to fight," Diane said in the same matter-of-factly way she had mentioned their low population numbers.

"But we need you here," the EC said. "You're our liaison. Besides, you're not warriors."

"From where do you think the d'solle come?"

Sky has suspected as much. Not for the entire quad, maybe, but for Diane. She was a large as the warriors, at least.

The four d'solle marched out of the conference room. Creighton took a step as if to stop them, but he gave that up and moved out of the way.

More sounds of big guns reached them, then the shouts of men and women.

"What do we do now?" Lars asked.

"Just what the colonel said. We stay right here," Sky responded. "Everyone, come here to the middle of the room and sit down."

EC Stanislaw was standing, his mouth gaping open. Sky was not the most senior member of the room by far, but the situation was new territory, and someone had to take charge. She grabbed the EC by his arm and led him to the center, then sat him down.

"Everyone, over here, now!" she ordered, and to her surprise, they all complied.

This isn't much, but it's the best we can do right now. Colonel, we're waiting for your Marine security.

Fifteen humans, supposedly among the best and brightest on the planet, sat there huddled while outside, Marines and soldiers joined the battle.

Chapter 36
Hondo

"Come on, come on," Hondo shouted at his fire team. "Get a move on!"

The entire battalion had returned to berthing at a dead run, shucked their utilities, and donned their long johns. Squads of Marines were already bolting to the armory to get into their PICS.

Each of the combat suits had been powered up for the up-check prior to turnover tomorrow, so CWO4 Donaldson and Staff Sergeant Jardine should be able to get the suits online within an hour--if the Grubs would give them the time. Even as they rushed to get ready, over 200 of the Grubs had landed on the planet with more landing every few minutes.

Three-Six had to join the fight. Two of the new battalions had already completed their PICS swap and were out in the training ranges getting a feel for their suits—now Two-Sixteen was locked into battle.

"Done!" Fiona shouted, and the four Marines—Hondo, BK, Fiona, and Aaron Manuel, who came over from Third Team—broke into a sprint to the armory. With only 12 donning stations, there was a line of Marines waiting. The flashing lights in the night sky reflected the urgency of the situation. Two-Sixteen was getting slaughtered.

"Let's hope First Tanks gets underway soon," Fiona said.

BK blanched. Gabriella was with First Tanks, a battalion now whittled down to 41 Mannies. Along with Marine Air, the tanks offered their best hope.

Another 12 Marines rushed in while the racks brought their PICS forward.

"How did the Grubs find us?" BK asked.

"Followed us back, I imagine," Sergeant Mbangwa said. "Now we've got to stop them."

"We've got a hell of a lot more Marines and Confeds here than we had on 3363," Paul said.

"But Two-Sixteen's just snapping in, and we've don't have enough PICS for everyone," BK said.

"But we're Jaegers, the toughest sons-of-bitches in the Corps. And we know a thing or two about fighting Grubs," the sergeant reminded them. "This is what we do."

"Ooh-rah, Sergeant!" BK and Hondo said in unison.

Hondo was kidding himself. With something like 200 on the planet, more now, most likely, and without a plan in place, this was going to be a tough fight. But, they'd beaten the bastards before, and they could do it again.

"Next twelve!" Staff Sergeant Jardine shouted, and Hondo stepped up to the fourth station.

He scanned his wrist, and the racking system shot down into the racks, emerging a few moments later with his PICS. A Marine he didn't recognize, probably from one of the incoming battalions, was there to help him.

He didn't need it. With a hop and twist that belied his bulk, he slipped into the familiar confines of his PICS.

"Didn't think I'd see you again," he muttered to his PICS as he snapped in and activated his readouts.

"Emergency check-list only," the Marine yelled at him as he snapped shut the back.

The ECL powered up a PICS in 30 seconds, bypassing 34 of the 52 components. It was enough to keep him fighting, but skipped some redundant functions or ones that could be ignored for the short term. The piss-snake, for example, took a minute on its own to connect and up-check. By skipping that, he'd be ready all the sooner. If his bladder let go, he might be uncomfortable, but he'd still be combat effective.

"You're green," a voice said through his comms. "Get off the station."

Hondo stepped back and waited in the staging area, eyes glued to the flickering lights in the near distance, as the rest of the squad came out. Throughout his short career so far, Hondo had been trained for a war where shielding, spoofing, and surveillance counter-measures made locating the enemy half of the battle. With the Grubs, there was no doubt as to where they were, especially in the dark. The flashes of light were beacons—as well as evidence of Marines dying.

"First Squad, to the spacepad," Sergeant Mbangwa passed. "We're going to be lifted to the far side of the battle. We need to relieve the pressure and draw the Grubs away from mainside. I'll give you more guidance as I get it myself."

The squad, light by five members and with barely two full fire teams, broke into their ground devouring trot to the spacepad ten short klicks down the gentle slope. All around them, the night shadows were rife with movement, other squads trotting alongside of them.

"OK, an update," the sergeant passed. "We're going to be lifted here," he said, as a position on Hondo's battlefield display highlighted. "We're to link up with one of the Kluck battalions that's on its way, then just like 3363, we're going to fix them and then let the Klucks roll up their flanks. Depending on how the Klucks do, we'll try to lead whatever Grubs are left away from mainside along this axis."

An arrow appeared, leading up the valley towards the higher hills 50 klicks away.

"I know this is kinda simplistic, so just keep your ears open and be ready to adjust as the battle demand."

"Par for the course," BK said, trotting beside him. "Not much in the details."

"Hooking us up with the Klucks, though, with this little notice, that's not half bad."

"I still want to know how the hell they found us. I mean, like, we're a long way from 3363, and they bypassed a shitload of Kluck worlds to get here."

"Like Paul said, they probably followed us back."

"Man, that's what the Brotherhood fucks and the other cowards were saying, that we're gonna lead the Grubs to human space."

Hell, she's right. The Brotherhood's going to go ballistic over this.

They passed the last of the mainside buildings, the spacepad in sight when a different type of light caught Hondo's attention. High above them, large spheres were descending.

His first thought was that these were larger versions of the light spheres that threw tendrils at the Marines, but Dixie said, "Shit, that's the Grubs coming in for a landing."

And things snapped into place. The "spheres" were Grubs, pulled into themselves, with no polyps, tentacles, and importantly, no light tendrils shooting down on them. Forty or fifty of them were descending, each one surrounded by a yellowish glow instead of their normal blue-whitish light.

"Hold up, Kilo," Lieutenant Copek ordered. "Weapons Pack 3, fire your M-56s."

Hondo automatically moved to his normal position in a halt, even if the threat was up above and descending. To his side, Aaron, deployed his M-56 and fired. The missile rose in a half-arc, streaking up to hit one of the Grubs. There was a huge fireball, and emerging out if it, the Grub continued to descend, looking untouched. More and more explosions lit the night sky, but not a single Grub looked to be hurt, much less killed.

"Cease fire, cease fire," the lieutenant passed. "We're just wasting missiles."

There was a rush of air, and Hondo spun about, ready to fire his own 20mm, but it was a Navy Shrike sweeping in. Hondo held his breath, waiting for the plane to be knocked out of the sky, but it flew right at the Grubs unimpeded, firing its beamers—and scoring hits. Two Grubs seemed to implode in a shower of sparks, as pretty as a Marine Corps Birthday fireworks display.

"Get some, squid!" BK shouted.

Hondo was puzzled that the Grubs weren't attacking the Shrike as it swept up and began a turn to hit them again. True, a Shrike was a far more robust craft than a Marine Falcon-C, but still, the Grubs should have reacted.

Unless they couldn't!

Incongruously and out of the blue, Hondo had remembered a World of Animals show where they said a skunk cannot spray unless it has its feet on the ground where it can brace them. What if the Grubs have to be on the ground, too? That would explain why they were featureless spheres and why they were letting the Navy Shrike strafe them.

"Staff Sergeant, I don't think they can fight when they're coming in. Look, no polyps," he passed to the acting platoon commander.

"Shit, I think you're right. Wait one."

A few moments later, the lieutenant passed, "As soon as the Grubs are within range of the grappling hooks and flames, light them up!"

"Good observation, Soldier," Sergeant Mbangwa passed on the P2P.

High above the first group of Grubs, additional lights began to appear. More were coming.

The Shrike pilot made another pass, this time plane's beamers crisping three more. That was a total of five—out of maybe 40. Hondo couldn't even tell how high they were. Depth perception was off in the darkness, and as featureless spheres, there was nothing to give contrast. He brought up his 20mm grenade launcher and tried to sight the nearest of the Grubs, but the rangefinder kept vacillating back and forth between 30 and 2600 meters.

"Kilo, pull back 500 meters at the double-time," Lieutenant Copek ordered.

With the Grubs drifting down, it was obvious why the company was given the order. The Marines had to get between the Grubs and mainside. Hondo's display suddenly indicated positions for every Marine—they'd been "AI'ed." Without time to do it himself, the lieutenant had given his battle AI a general intent, and that AI had picked spots for every Marine and sailor in the battalion, taking fire teams, the terrain, weapons coverage, and the approaching enemy into consideration. Marines didn't like to rely on AIs as a rule, despite their many proven advantages, but in this case, there was no choice.

Within 40 seconds, Hondo was sliding to a stop at his designated position, spinning around to face the Grubs. He could see their lateral motion now, so they had to be getting close. Using his night vision, he zoomed in to try and see any sign of life, but the Grubs were motionless inside their cocoon-like space ships.

Just stay asleep after you land, guys.

To his left, a stream of flame shot up, falling way short of its target. Someone had jumped the gun, not that Hondo blamed him or her. It was difficult to wait.

The Shrike buzzed the Grubs over Kilo again, racking up two more kills. That wasn't enough. The company had faced far fewer Grubs in its AOR on 3363, and the butcher's bill had been high.

Another flame reached out, this time tickling the edge of one of the lowest Grubs. The shielding/space ship/aura, whatever it was, glowed a deeper orange for a moment, but kept descending.

"Engage at will," Lieutenant Copek passed.

Hondo fired his grappling hook, half-expecting the yellow glow to bounce it back down, but the hook penetrated into the Grubs body before discharging. The Grub jerked, but not much else.

Within moments, every Grub was hit by hooks or had its sphere covered in flames. Two of the flaming spheres collapsed into sparks. Hondo hoped the rest were dead as well, just waiting to hit the ground.

About 80 meters away, the first of them landed, and almost immediately, the yellow light shifted to the familiar whitish-blue. Within seconds, the body sort of unrolled into the caterpillar shape, polyps shot out to tentacle length, and light tendrils whipped the area like a weedwhacker. One Marine fell while the single Grub lit up the area in actinic light.

It wasn't alone for long. Other Grubs landed; some came out light blazing, a few seemed to have problems generating much of anything, and more than a few were motionless. Three of the Grubs did their light merging thing, and as the Shrike came streaking in, the single beam reached out and hit it, sending it careening off course.

Hondo expected the Navy plane to go down, but that didn't make it any easier to accept.

"First Squad, on me," Sergeant Mbangwa passed as he highlighted a Grub that was moving toward Paul and First Fire Team.

Hondo and his three Marines shifted toward the squad leader. Around him, the NCOs, the backbone of the Corps, were taking over the fight, maneuvering their small units to engage the remaining Grubs.

The problem was that there were only seven squads left in the depleted Kilo Company, and at least 20 Grubs were still alive.

First Squad, Second Platoon, closed in with the nearest grub. Hondo loaded his spare hook as he rushed forward. He got kissed with a light tendril, but it seemed as if the Grub was a little confused with each of the Marines coming in from different angles. It didn't focus any of the light tendrils long enough to deplete any single PICS' shielding. Hondo fired, and when his hook, along with two others, slammed into it, it sort of sucked into itself, only one tendril flailing around. Fiona stepped closer and flamed it, the jelly-like fuel sticking to its side as it burned. Hondo allowed himself a moment to watch the flames dance, then smiled as the inevitable Grub explosion, even if that knocked down his shielding by another 8%.

"No time to admire our work. Shift," the sergeant ordered as he highlighted their new target.

They ran around Second Squad, which was engaged with another Grub. It was difficult to ignore their instincts to join in and help, but there were too many of the enemy on the ground. Their next target didn't look as robust as the rest, and as they charged forward, a single wavering light tendril reached out and latched on Dixie.

Hondo fired his 20mm grenades, not that they'd proven effective in the past but more to hopefully occupy the Grub's attention. He didn't have another hook, so it was pike time.

"I'm down to forty-two percent! Get it off my ass," Dixie shouted over her external mic, her normal comms blocked by the light tendril that still had her in its grip.

Hondo pulled the pike off its cradle on his back shoulder and then charged the Grub. With the single light tendril on Dixie, he had an unimpeded approach, and he rammed the pike home, activating its charge. Someone else hit it a few meters to the side as Hondo jumped back.

"Flame!" Jirly Dula shouted as she fired, enveloping the Grub.

Hondo darted back to put some distance between him and it before it blew. Still, the thing's explosion reduced his shielding by another 4%.

He felt the familiar surge of exultation, something he knew only a soldier could ever experience. His squad—his depleted squad—had just killed two of the Grubs. Maybe they'd get out of this in one piece after all.

He rushed forward and recovered his pike, which looked none the worse for wear. Whether it still had a charge was left to be seen, however.

"Check Dixie!" BK shouted as she rushed to the motionless Marine.

Hondo looked up, and he felt the crushing blow to the pit of his stomach. He didn't need to get closer to know that Dixie's PICS had been slagged. She was KIA.

"No time, BK," the sergeant passed. "We're not done here."

BK hesitated, looking at the mess that had been Dixie, then turned to join the others as Sergeant Mbangwa designated their next target, a Grub that was firing to the northwest. As Hondo ran forward, he caught a glimpse as to why. Thirty or forty Klethos were in full charge, and the dozen or so Grubs in the area were focused on them, ignoring the Marines.

All the better, Hondo thought, as he closed in.

"Kilo, listen up. New orders," the lieutenant passed. "Stop all fighting. Lima and we are to go back to mainside immediately. Platoon commanders, prepare for follow-on orders, but for now, get your Marines to the conference center. That means now! Pull back now!"

Hondo pulled to a stop, confused. His target was right there, only 150 meters away. He looked around, wondering if he could stick the Grub, then pull back.

"Don't even think about it, Soldier. You heard the skipper. Get your team and head back," Sergeant Mbangwa passed on the P2P as if he could read his intentions.

Hondo looked up. At least a hundred more lights had appeared. India and Mike couldn't hope to hold out against that, even with the Klethos' help. It didn't seem right to just abandon them.

"Now, Soldier. You've got your orders."

Fuck me royal!

"On me," he passed on the fire team circuit as he wheeled about and started in his PICS trot back to mainside.

The other three close in on him as by fire teams and squads, both companies coalesced as they ran. Hondo checked the numbers and winced. Somehow, First Squad had managed to kill two Grubs, even if one had been hurt, while losing only Dixie. At a quick glance, the rest of the two companies had not done as well. Their numbers were just over half of what they'd been only twenty minutes prior.

"Pick up the pace," Lieutenant Copek passed. "We've got a time crunch."

Time crunch? For what? We've got Grubs falling out of the sky on our heads.

Hondo moved out of trot and into run mode as the mass of Marines surged forward . . .

. . . and 18 Grubs landed just ahead and to their right. They unrolled and came up firing, engaging what was left of Third Platoon. Hondo automatically started to adjust course to help them, his fire team following, when Staff Sergeant Aster shouted "Stay the course" over the platoon net.

Hondo glanced to his left where Paul had started to lead his remaining Marine to the Grubs as well. Paul gave the

"PICS' shrug" of raising both gauntlets to shoulder level before he turned back to mainside just ahead.

Hondo was filled with a sense of frustration . . . and guilt. Marines were fighting and dying, and yet he was running away. Orders were orders, though, and discipline was a hallmark of the Corps.

"Keep going," he passed to the other three.

They reached the first outbuilding, fewer than a hundred of them left. Marines and soldiers, none of them in combat suits, were rushing forward, carrying a hodgepodge of weapons. One of them, a second lieutenant, jumped up in front of Hondo's team, yelling at him to turn around and fight, not run, and it killed a part of his very soul to ignore the lieutenant and run past him.

The fire team was one of the first to reach the conference center. After the mad rush to get there, no one knew what to do until a disheveled colonel stepped out of the building, an earbud and throat mic in place.

"Marines," he started. "We've got civilians inside, civilians that need to get off-planet now. You are going to take them. We've got shuttles coming in for bobo extracts, and you've got to get them there."

"That's bullshit!" someone passed.

"I'm giving you an . . ." he bristled before he stopped, seemed to get a hold of himself, and in a much calmer voice, said, "Look. I know it sounds bad, but these are the brain trust that knows more about the Grubs than anyone else. They've got to get off the planet if we're going to be able to carry on. These are the guys who've given us the hooks, the flamethrowers, and everything that has worked so far. This is a top priority."

He paused again, looking at the gathered Marines. "Any questions?"

There was none, so he asked, "Who's the senior Marine here?"

"I think I am, sir," Captain Lyle-Quisenberry , the Lima Company commander said.

"OK, Captain, I'm sending them out, about sixty of them. One to a Marine, and then get them to LZ Tern."

"You heard the colonel. Lieutenant Dockery, get your Marines up here. The rest of you, form a perimeter until your unit is called forward."

Hondo placed his team by the front hatch to the center as one of Lima's platoons came forward. One by one, civilians came out and climbed or were helped to onto the backs of the Marines. A PICS had two handles made for the purpose, and by standing on the hip flanges, a person should be able to ride a PICS Marine anywhere. At least a Marine could. These were civilians, and some were not in good shape, mentally or physically. A few had to have their hands strapped in, and one of those civilian's feet slipped the moment her Marine stepped off. She screamed as she dangled, wristed tied to the handles, but the Marine didn't stop. Her panic didn't matter as much as getting the woman to the incoming shuttles.

Within ten minutes, the bulk of the civilians had exited the center.

"How many left, sir?" Staff Sergeant Aster asked.

The lieutenant colonel assisting the full bird looked inside the hatch, then said, "Three more, Staff Sergeant."

"You're up, McKeever."

"BK, front and center."

BK stepped up and turned around while a fit-looking man climbed up. Without a word, BK took off at a trot, which made it more difficult for the man to stay on, but he managed.

Aaron took the next woman, and with one more civilian left, Hondo motioned for Fiona.

"I've still got my flamethrower and you don't have another hook, Corporal. You take her while I provide security."

Hondo wanted to object, but Fiona was right. He stepped up to the stairs so the woman could climb on.

To his surprise, it was the same woman he'd carried before, what seemed like decades ago, back on that first still unnamed planet.

"It's you, Doctor Ybarra," he blurted out.

"McKeever? Lance Corporal McKeever?" she asked, sounding equally surprised.

"Yes, ma'am. It's me. Corporal McKeever, now."

"Well, wonders never cease. Last time, I think you carried me. I don't think that'll be necessary now."

Hondo gave her his back, and he barely felt anything as she climbed on.

"Sir, are you ready to go?" Sergeant Mbangwa asked the colonel.

He and the lieutenant colonel laughed together before the colonel said, "You're here for the brain trust, not old farts like us. No, we'll stay here and fight. Now get out of here. You don't have much time."

Hondo stepped off, trying to keep his gait smooth, with Fiona, Sergeant Mbangwa, and Staff Sergeant Aster flanking him. They ran down the main drag, then cut between the barracks over to the perimeter road. LZ Tern was an alternate landing zone, designed for excess parking if needed. It was also just to the south of mainside, on the opposite side from where the Grubs were attacking.

Marines and soldiers were everywhere, few with any degree of armor, but all ready to fight if the expressions on their faces meant anything. Hondo had to slide to a stop when two Mannies passed in front of him as they rushed to the fight. Hondo wondered if BK's Gabriella was in one of them.

With a rush of sound, a shuttle shot into the air ahead of him. A load of civilians had just taken off. A "bobo" extract was a seat-of-the-pants effort. No air traffic control, no procedural niceties. It was shuttle in, shuttle out, any way it could. This shuttle seemed to turn back on itself, turning almost upside down as it dove back towards the ground. Hondo expected to see a plume of smoke from a crash, but the shuttle started to right itself before it disappeared from view behind some buildings. He knew then that the pilot was taking the shuttle ground-hugging until he or she felt safe enough to turn it over to the AI to get it up in orbit and to whatever waiting ship there was up there.

"Step it up, Soldier," Mbangwa said. "There's only one more shuttle."

He ran around the curve in the road, and there below him, 300 meters away, another shuttle was approaching the LZ.

He left the road to cut across the open area when Fiona said, "We've got company, Sergeant."

He should be focused on the LZ, but he couldn't help swinging around to see. Six Grubs were almost on top of them. Fiona ran forward flaming, enveloping one of them. All six hit the deck and unrolled, even the one she'd flamed.

Two of them converged their light, and the beam shot out to hit her.

Hondo took a step toward them, forgetting Dr. Ybarra on his back.

Sergeant Mbangwa grabbed his arm, swinging him around.

"Get her to the shuttle, now!"

He hesitated only a second as the sergeant and staff sergeant rushed to meet the Grubs.

It killed him, but the sergeant was right. Without another look, he broke into burst mode, almost flying down the gentle slope to the LZ. Civilians were crowding up the shuttle's ramp, as were more than a few Marines. A gunny was waving an arm, urging them to hurry.

Hondo slid to a stop, ready to shuck the doctor off his back.

"This is the last one!" he told the gunny.

"Just get aboard!" the gunny shouted.

"I'm going back!"

"No, you're not. You're to provide security for as long as it takes. Now get aboard now!"

Almost against his will, his traitorous legs obeyed the gunny and marched up the ramp. He ducked at the top, mindful of the woman on his back, and as he did, he managed a look back, the image forever seared into his mind.

Only a single Marine was standing, a Marine he knew was the Shona *Youmambo*, facing six Grubs. His PICS was burning with whitish-blue light, yet somehow, he was still moving forward.

Before the ramp closed, the shuttle jumped into the air, turned like the other had done, and bolted for safety. Hondo scrambled to maintain his balance and not crush the doctor. He caught the briefest glimpse of a Confederation Orcus rushing past as the shuttle's flight path smoothed out.

Hondo knew he could still pull up his combat display to see what happened to Fiona, the sergeant, and the staff sergeant. Instead, he powered the display down. He didn't want to confirm what he already knew.

He was vaguely aware of Dr. Ybarra thanking him, of BK coming over to sit beside him. There wasn't much he could do anymore. It was up to the shuttle pilot and AI now.

The rush of combat adrenaline now disappeared, and he was mentally and physically exhausted. He was numb.

Down on the planet's surface, his brothers and sisters were fighting and dying. Here he was, with a few others, somehow granted a golden ticket. He should be happy, relieved. He wasn't.

One thing was for sure, however. This war wasn't over. He'd have a chance to extract revenge, and he swore an oath right then that he'd achieve that.

The Grubs had better stand the fuck by.

CS MILAN

Chapter 37
Skylar

Sky lay in her rack, trying to sleep. She only had it for six hours—"hot-racking" they called it—before she'd have to give it up for the next person.

The Confederation ship was packed with four times her normal complement, and now it was returning to San Gregorio via a round-about route, chosen to throw off possible Grub tracking. From that small planet, other ships would take people to their final destinations.

For Sky, that meant Earth. The vice minister had already called her, congratulating her on what she'd achieved, and telling her she was expected back in Brussels. Sky didn't feel like she deserved congratulations. She'd been packed up like so much cargo and carried off Purgamentium by Corporal McKeever, Hondo, she'd found out was his first name.

She knew she was lucky. There had been close to 100,000 people on the planet before the Dictymorphs attacked with another 6,000 in orbit. Half of those in orbit and only 11,000 of those on the planet made it off alive—10,942, to be exact. The number was burned into her head.

There had almost assuredly been survivors of the attack, people who made it into the wilderness. People killed by the UAM.

With tens of thousands of Dictymorphs on the planet, the UAM had authorized a planet buster strike, the first one since the Soldiers of God homeworld 150 years ago. The Brotherhood, although not a participant in the war effort, had demanded it. With the concurrence of the Klethos-lee, the Secretary General had given the order, and the planet was hit with not one, but five of the planet busters, turning Purgamentium into a glowing ball of gas and rubble. The surveillance ships saw no signs of escaping Dictymorphs.

Some of the surviving Klethos made it off the planet before the strike, but any surviving humans not yet rescued were lost. The undernet was abuzz with the story of a New Budapest rapier pilot who swopped into the mountains north of the main bases to pull out four Confed soldiers just before the strike, his small craft damaged by the blast wave as it fled the doomed planet. The soldiers were the last four saved.

Sky had only casually wondered about her future. They'd suffered a huge defeat, and she was part of that. She knew it was possible that she could have received some of the blame. It had happened often enough before. But oddly enough, she hadn't been concerned about that. If it happened, it happened.

But the vice-minister had been pretty clear. Her star was rising, and she was to return to a promotion and a position of higher authority.

Just as she hadn't been too concerned about getting punished, neither could she get excited about the promotion. At best she was ambivalent.

She'd do the job, and do whatever it took to defeat the Dictymorphs. This was now cemented into her DNA, something that she knew was going to take every waking moment until the *Grubs* were destroyed, wiped from the galaxy. It was just that she took no real pride in anything. Too many people, good people, had been lost for her to feel anything like that. But just like breathing and eating, she couldn't escape her mission even if she wanted to.

And she didn't want to.

She checked her PA. She still had three hours left of rack time, but she knew she wasn't going to use it. She might as well vacate it for her next rack-mate. She swung her legs over the edge of the rack and slid out, landing lightly on the deck. Hitting the small green button on the head of the bunk, she let her rack-mates know it was free.

With so much surveillance over and on the planet, there were more recordings than she could ever hope to see. She wanted to watch the Dictymorphs land again to see if something new would catch her eye. She'd planned on starting on that in another day or so, but there was nothing like the present to get going.

Sky slid her feet into her ship's slippers stepped out of the berthing, closing the hatch behind her.

ITZUKO-2
Camp Fiona Xeras

Epilogue
Hondo

Sergeant Hondo McKeever looked into the mirror, checking his uniform for the slightest imperfection. He wanted to make a good impression.

He'd never thought he'd be a Drill Instructor. He'd never wanted to be one. But the needs of the Corps trumped anything else, and what the Corps needed now was experienced instructors.

A cloud passed through his mind as the thought hit him, but he brushed it aside. It was easier now than it had been for the first few months after Purgamentium. Corps-wide, there were slightly over 5,000 Marines with combat experience against the Grubs, and they were a vital and valuable commodity. Three thousand of them had already transferred by the time of the Grub attack, and another two had managed to get off the planet during and after the attack. That left 5,000 Marines and Navy corpsmen to train the next wave of Marines.

And the wave was a tsunami. The Federation was officially on a war footing. For the first time since the War of the Far Reaches, the Federation had instituted a draft. Over a million young men and women had already been inducted, and the first recruit training graduates were about to start infantry training. And that was where combat vets like Hondo fit in.

Sitting (nervously, he knew) in Classroom A, were 492 recently graduated Marine privates. Boot camp, with all the stress associated with it, was over. But now, the hard part was about to begin. Failing boot camp meant disgrace and a trip back home. Failing infantry training meant dying in battle and getting fellow Marines killed. It was up Hondo to keep that from happening.

Every one of those 492 privates would see battle, Hondo knew. The Grubs were out there, and they were coming. The Marines, Navy, and the other forces in the coalition were all that stood between survival and genocide.

Hondo would rather be at the point of the spear. He wanted to try out the new weapons pouring out of the Alley, the nickname for the huge research facility built on 700 klicks north of Camp Xeras. But deep down, he knew why he was going to be stuck as a School of Infantry DI, teaching Module 1. Gunny Leung was technically the senior instructor, but Hondo was the key player. He had the street cred.

Finally satisfied with his appearance, he left his small room, walked across the passage, and knocked on the hatch.

"You ready?"

"Sure am, Sergeant," Corporal BK Dodds, said as she opened her hatch.

The two Marines left the barracks and walked across the quad towards the classrooms. They stopped, however, halfway across, at the plaque bolted to the big rock just in front of the flagpole.

They looked at it, neither saying a word. It was still shiny, unblemished by weather.

Camp Fiona L. Xeras
Named in Honor of Lance Corporal Fiona L. Xeras,
United Federation Marine Corps
Holder of the United Assembly of Man Gold Starburst
KIA 4 September 433
Battle of K-3393

Hondo still felt a lump in his throat when he looked at the plaque. It was not just for Fiona, but for all of them. Sergeant Mbangwa. Sunrise. Sam. Doc Pataki. Rosy. Dixie. Loren. Brute. Tinman. Staff Sergeant Aster. Lieutenant Silas. And so many more. Brothers and sisters, all lost for the cause.

He reached over with his thumb and rubbed Fiona's name.

Rest in Peace, Marine.

"OK, BK, let's go train some Marines."

The two friends pulled their head high, stood straight, and strode over to the classroom to begin their next mission.

Thank you for reading *Alliance*. I hope you enjoyed this book, and I welcome a review on Amazon, Goodreads, or any other outlet.

If you would like updates on new books releases, news, or special offers, please consider signing up for my mailing list. Your email will not be sold, rented, or in any other way disseminated. If you are interested, please sign up at the link below:

http://eepurl.com/bnFSHH

Other Books by Jonathan Brazee

The United Federation Marine Corps' Lysander Twins

Legacy Marines
Esther's Story: Recon Marine
Noah's Story: Marine Tanker
Esther's Story: Special Duty
Blood United

Coda

The United Federation Marine Corps

Recruit
Sergeant
Lieutenant
Captain
Major
Lieutenant Colonel
Colonel
Commandant

Rebel
(Set in the UFMC universe.)

Behind Enemy Lines
(A UFMC Prequel)

Women of the United Federation Marine Corps
Gladiator
Sniper
Corpsman

High Value Target (A Gracie Medicine Crow Short Story)
BOLO Mission (A Gracie Medicine Crow Short Story)
Weaponized Math

The United Federation Marine Corps' Grub Wars
Alliance
Civil War (Working title—coming soon)

The Return of the Marines Trilogy
The Few
The Proud
The Marines

The Al Anbar Chronicles: First Marine Expeditionary Force--Iraq
Prisoner of Fallujah
Combat Corpsman
Sniper

Werewolf of Marines
Werewolf of Marines: Semper Lycanus
Werewolf of Marines: Patria Lycanus
Werewolf of Marines: Pax Lycanus

Jonathan P. Brazee

To The Shores of Tripoli

Wererat

Darwin's Quest: The Search for the Ultimate Survivor

Venus: A Paleolithic Short Story

Secession

Duty

Non-Fiction

Exercise for a Longer Life

Author Website
http://www.jonathanbrazee.com

Made in the USA
Columbia, SC
28 October 2024